TOPLINERS
GENERAL EDITOR: AIDAN CHAMBERS

Ghosts 4

For this, the fourth collection of Topliner ghost stories,
Malcolm Blacklin has brought together some of his
favourite fearsome apparitions, ghastly phantoms and
bloodcurdling manifestations from the candle-lit days of
the last century. Some of the stories are accounts of
ghosts people claim to have seen; three stories are
fictional – ghosts that haunted their writers' imaginations.
Fact or fiction, the stories in this book are not for
readers who are easily scared. Read on at your peril. . . .

TOPLINERS

Ghosts 4

Compiled by Malcolm Blacklin

Macmillan

Selection and introductions
© Malcolm Blacklin 1978

All rights reserved. No part of this publication
may be reproduced or transmitted, in any form or
by any means, without permission.

First published 1978

Published in *Topliners* by
MACMILLAN EDUCATION LIMITED
Houndmills Basingstoke Hampshire RG21 2XS
and London
Associated companies in Delhi Dublin
Hong Kong Johannesburg Lagos Melbourne
New York Singapore and Tokyo

Printed in Hong Kong

Topliners are sold subject to the condition that
they shall not, by way of trade or otherwise, be lent, resold,
hired out or otherwise circulated without the publisher's
prior consent, in any form of binding or cover other than
that in which they are published and without a similar
condition, including this condition, being imposed on the
subsequent purchaser.

British Library Cataloguing in Publication Data
Ghosts.
4. – (Topliners).
1. Ghost stories, English 2. Short stories,
English
I. Blacklin, Malcolm II. Series
823'.9'1FS   PR1309.G5

ISBN 0-333-24796-5

Contents

1	Dracula's Guest	1
2	Two Haunted Houses	18
3	The Gambling Ghosts	27
4	Something Wicked This Way Comes	31
5	A Ghost of the Future	51
6	Witness to Murder	55
7	The House of Death	83
8	Fact or Fiction?	91
9	The Voice in the Night	92
10	School for the Unspeakable	109

Acknowledgements

The compiler and publisher wish to thank the following who have kindly given permission for the use of copyright material:

Barrie & Jenkins Limited for an extract from *Ghosts I Have Seen* by Violet Tweedale;

Routledge & Kegan Paul Limited for an extract from *A Dictionary of British Folk Tales* by K. M. Briggs.

Every effort has been made to trace all the copyright holders but if any have been inadvertently overlooked the publishers will be pleased to make the necessary arrangement at the first opportunity.

1 Dracula's Guest

Ghosts, it seems to me, were at their best about a hundred years ago during the nineteenth century, before electricity arrived to brighten up our homes at night. Houses were gloomily lit, full of eerie shadows and dark nooks and crannies: just the sort of places ghosts thrive in. And, to be honest, I like my ghosts to be frightening – in stories anyway.

I think Bram Stoker must have agreed with me. He was the author of one of the most horrifying ghost stories ever written, *Dracula*, which appeared in 1897 and has been popular ever since. So I have chosen to begin this collection of stories about ghosts people claim to have seen, as well as those invented by writers just to scare us, with one of the most spectacular episodes from that novel.

Though Count Dracula, handsome nobleman and vicious vampire, was entirely a product of Bram Stoker's imagination, vampires have been around for a long time. Especially in mid-European countries, Russia and China, people often used to report being plagued by them. They are the strangest, most frightening ghosts of all: dead bodies that stay alive by sucking on living people's blood, thereby turning their victims into vampires too. Whether they really existed or not I do not know, but Bram Stoker makes me believe they did – at least, while I am reading his story.

WALPURGISNACHT
by Bram Stoker

When we started for our drive the sun was shining

brightly on Munich, and the air was full of the joyousness of early summer. Just as we were about to depart, Herr Delbrück (the maître d'hôtel of the Quatre Saisons, where I was staying) came down, bareheaded, to the carriage and, after wishing me a pleasant drive, said to the coachman, still holding his hand on the handle of the carriage door,

'Remember you are back by nightfall. The sky looks bright, but there is a shiver in the north wind that says there may be a sudden storm. But I am sure you will not be late.' Here he smiled, and added, 'For you know what night it is.'

Johann answered with an emphatic, '*Ja, mein Herr,*' and, touching his hat, drove off quickly. When we had cleared the town, I said, after signalling to him to stop, 'Tell me, Johann, what is tonight?'

He crossed himself, as he answered laconically, '*Walpurgisnacht.*' Then he took out his watch, a great, old-fashioned German-silver thing as big as a turnip, and looked at it, with his eyebrows gathered together and a little impatient shrug of his shoulders. I realised that this was his way of respectfully protesting against the unnecessary delay, and sank back in the carriage, merely motioning him to proceed. He started off rapidly, as if to make up for lost time. Every now and then the horses seemed to throw up their heads and sniff the air suspiciously. On such occasions I often looked round in alarm. That road was pretty bleak, for we were traversing a sort of high, windswept plateau. As we drove, I saw a road that looked but little used, and which seemed to dip through a little winding valley. It looked so inviting that, even at the risk of offending him, I called Johann to stop. And when he had pulled up I told him I would like to drive down that road. He made all sorts of excuses, and frequently crossed himself as he spoke. This somewhat piqued my curiosity, so I asked him various questions. He answered fencingly, and repeatedly looked at his watch in protest.

Finally I said, 'Well, Johann, I want to go down this road. I shall not ask you to come unless you like; but tell me why you do not like to go, that is all I ask.'

For answer he seemed to throw himself off the box, so quickly did he reach the ground. Then he stretched out his hands appealing to me, and implored me not to go. There was just enough of English mixed with the German for me to understand the drift of his talk. He seemed always just about to tell me something – the very idea of which evidently frightened him; but each time he pulled himself up, saying, as he crossed himself, '*Walpurgisnacht!*'

I tried to argue with him, but it was difficult to argue with a man when I did not know his language. The advantage certainly rested with him, for although he began to speak in English – of a very crude and broken kind – he always got excited and broke into his native tongue – and every time he did so he looked at his watch. Then the horses became restless and sniffed the air. At this he grew very pale, and, looking around in a frightened way, he suddenly jumped forward, took them by the bridles and led them on some twenty feet. I followed, and asked why he had done this. For answer he crossed himself, pointed to the spot we had left, and drew his carriage in the direction of the other road, indicating a cross, and said, first in German, then in English, 'Buried him – him what killed themselves.'

I remembered the old custom of burying suicides at crossroads. 'Ah! I see, a suicide. How interesting!' But for the life of me I could not make out why the horses were frightened.

Whilst we were talking, we heard a sort of sound between a yelp and a bark. It was far away; but the horses got very restless, and it took Johann all his time to quiet them. He was pale, and said: 'It sounds like a wolf – but yet there are no wolves here now.'

'No?' I said, questioning him. 'Isn't it long since the wolves were so near the city?'

'Long, long,' he answered, 'in the spring and summer; but with the snow the wolves have been here not so long.'

Whilst he was petting the horses and trying to quiet them, dark clouds drifted rapidly across the sky. The sunshine passed away, and a breath of cold wind seemed to drift past us. It was only a breath, however, and more in the nature of a warning than a fact, for the sun came out brightly again.

Johann looked under his lifted hand at the horizon and said, 'The storm of snow, he comes before long time.' Then he looked at his watch again, and, straightway, holding his reins firmly – for the horses were still pawing the ground restlessly, and shaking their heads – he climbed to his box as though the time had come for proceeding on our journey.

I felt a little obstinate, and did not at once get into the carriage.

'Tell me,' I said, 'about this place where the road leads.' And I pointed down.

Again he crossed himself and mumbled a prayer, before he answered, 'It is unholy.'

'What is unholy?' I inquired.

'The village.'

'Then there is a village?'

'No, no. No one lives there hundreds of years.'

My curiosity was piqued. 'But you said there was a village.'

'There was.'

'Where is it now?'

Whereupon he burst out into a long story in German and English, so mixed up that I could not quite understand exactly what he said, but roughly I gathered that long ago, hundreds of years, men had died there and been buried in their graves; and sounds were heard under the clay, and when the graves were opened, men and women were found rosy with life, and their mouths red with blood. And so, in haste to save their lives (aye, and their souls! – and here he crossed himself), those who were left fled away to other places, where the living lived, and the dead were dead and not – not something. He was evidently afraid to speak the last words. As he proceeded with his narration, he grew more and more excited. It seemed as if his imagination had got hold of him, and he ended in a perfect paroxysm of fear – white-faced, perspiring, trembling and looking round him, as if expecting that some dreadful presence would manifest itself there in the bright sunshine on the open plain. Finally, in an agony of desperation, he cried,

'*Walpurgisnacht!*' and pointed to the carriage for me to get in. All my English blood rose at this, and, standing back, I said:

'You are afraid, Johann – you are afraid. Go home; I shall return alone; the walk will do me good.' The carriage door was open. I took from the seat my oak walking stick – which I always carry on my holiday excursions – and closed the door, pointing back to Munich, and said, 'Go home, Johann – *Walpurgisnacht* doesn't concern Englishmen.'

The horses were now more restive than ever, and Johann was trying to hold them in, while excitedly imploring me not to do anything so foolish. I pitied the poor fellow, he was so deeply in earnest; but all the same I could not help laughing. His English was quite gone now. In his anxiety he had forgotten that his only means of making me understand was to talk my language, so he jabbered away in his native German. It began to be a little tedious. After giving the direction, 'Home!' I turned to go down the crossroad into the valley.

With a despairing gesture, Johann turned his horses towards Munich. I leaned on my stick and looked after him. He went slowly along the road for a while; then there came over the crest of the hill a man tall and thin. I could see so much in the distance. When he drew near the horses, they began to jump and kick about, then to scream with terror. Johann could not hold them in; they bolted down the road, running away madly. I watched them out of sight, then looked for the stranger, but I found that he, too, was gone.

With a light heart I turned down the side road through the deepening valley to which Johann had objected. There was not the slightest reason, that I could see, for his objection; and I dare say I tramped for a couple of hours without thinking of time or distance, and certainly without seeing a person or a house. So far as the place was concerned, it was desolation itself. But I did not notice this particularly till, on turning a bend in the road, I came upon a scattered fringe of wood; then I recognised that I had been impressed unconsciously by the desolation of the region through which I had passed.

I sat down to rest myself, and began to look around.

It struck me that it was considerably colder than it had been at the commencement of my walk – a sort of sighing sound seemed to be around me, with, now and then, high overhead, a sort of muffled roar. Looking upwards, I noticed that great thick clouds were drifting rapidly across the sky from north to south at a great height. There were signs of coming storm in some lofty stratum of the air. I was a little chilly, and, thinking that it was the sitting still after the exercise of walking, I resumed my journey.

The ground I passed over was now much more picturesque. There were no striking objects that the eye might single out; but in all there was a charm of beauty. I took little heed of time and it was only when the deepening twilight forced itself upon me that I began to think of how I should find my way home. The brightness of the day had gone. The air was cold, and the drifting of clouds high overhead was more marked. They were accompanied by a sort of faraway rushing sound, through which seemed to come at intervals that mysterious cry which the driver had said came from a wolf. For a while I hesitated. I had said I would see the deserted village, so on I went, and presently came on a wide stretch of open country shut in by hills all around. Their sides were covered with trees, which spread down to the plain, dotting, in clumps, the gentler slopes and hollows which showed here and there. I followed with my eye the winding of the road, and saw that it curved close to one of the densest of these clumps and was lost behind it.

As I looked there came a cold shiver in the air, and the snow began to fall. I thought of the miles and miles of bleak country I had passed, and then hurried on to seek the shelter of the wood in front. Darker and darker grew the sky, and faster and heavier fell the snow, till the earth before and around me was a glistening white carpet the farther edge of which was lost in misty vagueness. The road was here but crude, and, when on the level, its boundaries were not so marked as when it passed through the cuttings; and in a little while I found that I must have strayed from it, for I missed underfoot the hard surface, and my feet sank deeper in the grass and moss. Then the wind grew stronger and blew with ever-increasing force, till I was fain to run before it. The air became icy cold, and in spite of my exercise I began to suffer. The snow was now falling so thickly and whirling around me in such rapid eddies that I could hardly keep my eyes open. Every now and then the heavens were torn asunder by vivid lightning, and in the flashes I could see ahead of me a great mass of trees, chiefly yew and cypress; all heavily coated with snow.

I was soon amongst the shelter of the trees, and there, in comparative silence, I could hear the rush of the wind high overhead. Presently the blackness of the storm had become merged in the darkness of the night. By and by the storm seemed to be passing away; it now only came in fierce puffs or blasts. At such moments the weird sound of the wolf appeared to be echoed by many similar sounds around me.

Now and again, through the black mass of drifting cloud, came a straggling ray of moonlight, which lit up the expanse, and showed me that I was at the edge of a dense mass of cypress and yew trees. As the snow had ceased to fall, I walked out from the shelter and began to investigate more closely. It appeared to me that, amongst so many old foundations as I had passed, there might be still standing a house in which, though in ruins, I could find some sort of shelter for a while. As I skirted the edge of the copse, I found that a low wall encircled it, and following this I presently found an opening. Here the cypresses formed an alley leading up to a square mass of some kind of building. Just as I caught sight of this, however, the drifting clouds obscured the moon, and I passed up the path in darkness. The wind must have grown colder, for I felt myself shiver as I walked; but there was hope of shelter, and I groped my way blindly on.

I stopped, for there was a sudden stillness. The storm had passed; and, perhaps in sympathy with Nature's silence, my heart seemed to cease to beat. But this was only momentarily; for suddenly the moonlight broke through the clouds, showing me that I was in a graveyard, and that the square object before me was a great massive tomb of marble, as white as the snow that lay on and all around it. With the moonlight there came a fierce sigh of the storm, which appeared to resume its course with a long, low howl, as of many dogs or wolves. I was awed and shocked, and felt the cold perceptibly grow upon me till it seemed to grip me by the heart. Then, while the flood of moonlight still fell on the marble tomb, the storm gave further evidence of renewing – as though it was returning on its track. Impelled by some sort of fascination, I approached the sepulchre to see what it was, and why such a thing stood alone in such a place. I walked around it, and read, over the Doric door, in German:

COUNTESS DOLINGER OF GRATZ
IN STYRIA
SOUGHT AND FOUND DEAD
1801

On the top of the tomb, seemingly driven through the solid marble – for the structure was composed of a few vast blocks of stone – was a great iron spike or stake. On going to the back I saw, graven in great Russian letters:

The dead travel fast.

There was something so weird and uncanny about the whole thing that it gave me a turn and made me feel quite faint. I began to wish, for the first time, that I had taken Johann's advice. Here a thought struck me, which came under almost mysterious circumstances and with a terrible shock. This was Walpurgis Night!

Walpurgis Night, when, according to the belief of millions of people, the devil was abroad – when the graves were opened and the dead came forth and walked. When all evil things of earth and air and water held revel. This very place the driver had specially shunned. This was the depopulated village of centuries ago. This was where the suicide lay; and this was the place where I was alone – unmanned, shivering with cold in a shroud of snow with a wild storm gathering again upon me! It took all my philosophy, all the religion I had been taught, all my courage, not to collapse in a paroxysm of fright.

And now a perfect tornado burst upon me. The ground shook as though thousands of horses thundered across it; and this time the storm bore on its icy wings, not snow, but great hailstones which drove with such violence that they might have come from the thongs of Balearic slingers – hailstones that beat down leaf and branch and made the shelter of the cypresses of no more avail than though their stems were standing corn. At the first I had rushed to the nearest tree; but I was soon fain to leave it and seek the only spot that seemed to afford refuge, the deep Doric doorway of the marble tomb. There, crouching against the massive bronze door, I gained a certain amount of protection from the beating of the hailstones, for now they only drove against me as they ricocheted from the ground and the side of the marble.

As I leaned against the door it moved slightly and opened inwards. The shelter of even a tomb was welcome in that pitiless tempest, and I was about to enter it when there came a flash of forked lightning that lit up the whole expanse of the heavens. In the instant, as I am a living man, I saw, as my eyes were turned into the darkness of the tomb, a beautiful woman, with rounded cheeks and red lips, seemingly sleeping on a bier. As the thunder broke overhead, I was grasped as by the hand of a giant and hurled out into the storm. The whole thing was so sudden that, before I could realise the shock, moral as well as physical, I found the hailstones beating me down. At the same time I had a strange, dominating feeling that I was not alone. I looked towards the tomb. Just then there came another blinding flash, which seemed to strike the iron stake that surmounted the tomb and to pour through to the earth, blasting and crumbling the marble, as in a burst of flame. The dead woman rose for a moment of agony, while she was lapped in the flame, and her bitter scream of pain was drowned in the thundercrash. The last thing I heard was this mingling of dreadful sound, as again I was seized in the giant grasp and dragged away, while the hailstones beat on me, and the air around seemed reverberant with the howling of wolves. The last sight that I remembered was a vague, white, moving mass, as if all the graves around me had sent out the phantoms of their sheeted dead, and they were closing in on me through the white cloudiness of the driving hail.

Gradually there came a sort of vague beginning of consciousness; then a sense of weariness that was dreadful. For a time I remembered nothing; but slowly my senses returned. My feet seemed positively racked with pain, yet I could not move them. They seemed to be numbed. There was an icy feeling at the back of my neck and all down my spine, and my ears, like my feet, were dead, yet in torment, but there was in my breast a sense of warmth which was, by comparison, delicious. It was as a nightmare – a physical nightmare, if one may use such an expression; for some heavy weight on my chest made it difficult for me to breathe.

This period of semi-lethargy seemed to remain a long time, and as it faded away I must have slept or swooned. Then came a sort of loathing, like the first stage of seasickness, and a wild desire to be free from something – I knew not what. A vast stillness enveloped me, as though all the world were asleep or dead – only broken by the low panting as of some animal close to me. I felt a warm rasping at my throat, then came a consciousness of the awful truth, which chilled me to the heart and sent the blood surging up through my brain. Some great animal was lying on me and now licking my throat. I feared to stir, for some instinct of prudence made me lie still; but the brute seemed to realise that there was now some change in me, for it raised its head. Through my eyelashes I saw above me the two great flaming eyes of a gigantic wolf. Its sharp white teeth gleamed in the gaping red mouth, and I could feel its hot breath fierce and acrid upon me.

For another spell of time I remembered no more. Then I became conscious of a low growl, followed by a yelp, renewed again and again. Then, seemingly very far away, I heard a 'Holloa! Holloa!' as of many voices calling in unison. Cautiously I raised my head and looked in the direction whence the sound came; but the cemetery blocked my view. The wolf still continued to yelp in a strange way, and a red glare began to move round the grove of cypresses, as though following the sound. As the voices drew closer, the wolf yelped faster and louder. I feared to make either sound or motion. Nearer came the red glow, over the white pall which stretched into the darkness around me. Then all at once from beyond the trees there came at a trot a troop of horsemen bearing torches. The wolf rose from my breast and made for the cemetery. I saw one of the horsemen (soldiers by their caps and their long military cloaks) raise his carbine and take aim. A companion knocked up his arm, and I heard the ball whiz over my head. He had evidently taken my body for that of the wolf. Another sighted the animal as it slunk away, and a shot followed. Then, at a gallop, the troop rode forward; some towards me, others following the wolf as it disappeared amongst the snow-clad cypresses.

As they drew nearer I tried to move, but was powerless, although I could see and hear all that went on around me. Two or three of the soldiers jumped from their horses and knelt beside me. One of them raised my head, and placed his hand over my heart.

'Good news, comrades!' he cried. 'His heart still beats!'

Then some brandy was poured down my throat; it put vigour into me, and I was able to open my eyes fully and look around. Lights and shadows were moving among the trees, and I heard men call to one another. They drew together uttering frightened exclamations; and the lights flashed as the others came pouring out of the cemetery pell-mell, like men possessed. When the farther ones came close to us, those who were around me asked them eagerly,

'Well, have you found him?'

The reply rang out hurriedly,

'No! No! Come away quick – quick! This is no place to stay, and on this of all nights!'

'What was it?' was the question, asked in all manner of keys. The answer came variously and all indefinitely as though the men were moved by some common impulse to speak, yet were restrained by some common fear from giving their thoughts.

'It – it – indeed!' gibbered one, whose wits had plainly given out for the moment.

'A wolf – and yet not a wolf!' another put in shudderingly.

'No use trying for him without the sacred bullet,' a third remarked in a more ordinary manner.

'Serve us right for coming out on this night! Truly we have earned our thousand marks!' were the ejaculations of a fourth.

'There was blood on the broken marble,' another said after a pause. 'The lightning never brought that there. And for him – is he safe? Look at his throat! See, comrades, the wolf has been lying on him and keeping his blood warm.'

The officer looked at my throat and replied,

'He is all right; the skin is not pierced. What does it all mean? We should never have found him but for the yelping of the wolf.'

'What became of it?' asked the man who was holding

up my head, and who seemed the least panic-stricken of the party, for his hands were steady and without tremor. On his sleeve was the chevron of a petty officer.

'It went to its home,' answered the man, whose long face was pallid, and who actually shook with terror as he glanced around him fearfully. 'There are graves enough there in which it may lie. Come, comrades – come quickly! Let us leave this cursed spot.'

The officer raised me to a sitting posture as he uttered a word of command; then several men placed me upon a horse. He sprang to the saddle behind me, took me in his arms, gave the word to advance; and, turning our faces away from the cypresses, we rode away in swift, military order.

As yet my tongue refused its office, and I was perforce silent. I must have fallen asleep; for the next thing I remembered was finding myself standing up, supported by a soldier on each side of me. It was almost broad daylight, and to the north a red streak of sunlight was reflected, like a path of blood, over the waste of snow. The officer was telling the men to say nothing of what they had seen, except that they found an English stranger, guarded by a large dog.

'Dog! That was no dog,' cut in the man who had exhibited such fear. 'I think I know a wolf when I see one.'

The young officer answered calmly, 'I said a dog.'

'Dog!' reiterated the other ironically. It was evident that his courage was rising with the sun; and, pointing to me, he said, 'Look at his throat. Is that the work of a dog, master?'

Instinctively I raised my hand to my throat, and as I touched it I cried out in pain. The men crowded round to look, some stooping down from their saddles; and again there came the calm voice of the young officer,

'A dog, as I said. If aught else were said we should only be laughed at.'

I was then mounted behind a trooper, and we rode on into the suburbs of Munich. Here we came across a stray carriage, into which I was lifted, and it was driven off to the Quatre Saisons – the young officer accompanying me, whilst a trooper followed with his horse, and the others rode off to their barracks.

When we arrived, Herr Delbrück rushed so quickly down the steps to meet me that it was apparent he had been watching within. Taking me by both hands he solicitously led me in. The officer saluted me and was turning to withdraw, when I recognised his purpose, and insisted that he should come to my rooms. Over a glass of wine I warmly thanked him and his brave comrades for saving me. He replied simply that he was more than glad, and that Herr Delbrück had at the first taken steps to make all the searching party pleased; at which ambiguous utterance the maître d'hôtel smiled, while the officer pleaded duty and withdrew.

'But Herr Delbrück,' I inquired, 'how and why was it that soldiers searched for me?'

He shrugged his shoulders, as if in depreciation of his own deed, as he replied,

'I was so fortunate as to obtain leave, from the commander of the regiment in which I served, to ask for volunteers.'

'But how did you know I was lost?' I asked.

'The driver came hither with the remains of his carriage, which had been upset when the horses ran away.'

'But surely you would not send a search party of soldiers merely on this account?'

'Oh no!' he answered. 'But even before the coachman arrived, I had this telegram from the Boyar whose guest you are,' and he took from his pocket a telegram, which he handed to me, and I read,

Bistrize.

Be careful of my guest—his safety is most precious to me. Should aught happen to him, or if he be missed, spare nothing to find him and ensure his safety. He is English and therefore adventurous. There are often dangers from snow and wolves and night. Lose not a moment if you suspect harm to him. I answer your zeal with my fortune.

DRACULA.

As I held the telegram in my hand, the room seemed to whirl around me; and, if the attentive maître d'hôtel had not caught me, I think I should have fallen. There was something so strange in all this, something so weird and impossible to imagine, that there grew on me a sense of my being in some way the sport of opposite forces – the mere vague idea of which seemed in a way to paralyse me. I was certainly under some form of mysterious protection. From a distant country had come, in the very nick of time, a message that took me out of the danger of the snow-sleep and the jaws of the wolf.

2 Two Haunted Houses

Not only were ghosts at their best in Victorian times, but nineteenth-century writers described them and their hauntings much more vividly than writers do now. Perhaps they believed in ghosts more completely; perhaps their style of writing suited ghosts better. These two stories will show you what I mean.

They come from my favourite collection of true-ghost accounts, *The Haunted Homes and Family Traditions of Great Britain*, by John H. Ingram, a fat book which has given me hours of pleasure. Ingram set the pattern for many of the ghost writers who followed him. His tales are a mixture of his own words and the letters, reports, conversations and published descriptions of people who witnessed ghostly events, or, at least, knew about them from their own investigations. (In fact, Ingram got the idea for his book from an even earlier one, *The Night Side of Nature* by Catherine Crowe, first published in 1853.)

Here are two from his collection. Each is typical of a kind of haunting found frequently, not only in Ingram's book but in all surveys of ghostly phenomena. By the way, the Victorians were coy about telling the public the names of people reporting ghosts or the sites of the hauntings. So the first story is by 'a young lady' described as 'intelligent'; the house where the events took place was 'an old mansion in the north of Yorkshire; cosy and cheerful, though large, and lonely'.

THE GHOSTLY GIRL
by 'A Young Lady'

What I am going to relate happened to myself while

staying with some north-country cousins, last July, at their house in Yorkshire. I had spent a few days there in the summer of the previous year, but without then hearing or seeing anything out of the common. On my second visit, arriving early in the afternoon, I went out boating with some of the family, spent a very jolly evening, and finally went to bed, a little tired, perhaps, with the day's work but not the least nervous. I slept soundly until between three and four, just when the day was beginning to break. I had been awake for a short time when suddenly the door of my bedroom opened, and shut again rather quickly. I fancied it might be one of the servants, and called out, 'Come in!' After a short time the door opened again, but no one came in – at least, no one that I could see.

Almost at the same time that the door opened for the second time, I was a little startled by the rustling of some curtains belonging to a hanging wardrobe, which stood by the side of the bed; the rustling continued, and I was seized with a most uncomfortable feeling, not exactly of fright, but a strange, unearthly sensation *that I was not alone*. I had had that feeling for some minutes, when I saw at the foot of the bed a child, about seven or nine years old. The child seemed as if it were on the bed, and came gliding towards me as I lay. It was the figure of a little girl in her nightdress – a little girl with dark hair and a very white face. I tried to speak to her, but could not. She came slowly on up to the top of the bed, and I then saw her face clearly. She seemed in great trouble; her hands were clasped and her eyes were turned up with a look of entreaty, an almost agonised look. Then, slowly unclasping her hands, she touched me on the shoulder. The hand felt icy-cold, and while I strove to speak she was gone.

I felt more frightened after the child was gone than before, and began to be very anxious for the time when the servant would make her appearance. Whether I slept again or not, I hardly know. But by the time the servant did come, I had almost persuaded myself that the whole affair was nothing but a very vivid nightmare. However, when I came down to breakfast, there were many remarks made about my not looking well – it was observed that I was pale. In answer I told my cousins that I had had a most vivid nightmare, and I remarked if I was a believer in ghosts I should imagine I had seen one. Nothing more was said at the time upon this subject, except that my host, who was a doctor, observed that I had better not sleep in the room again, at any rate not alone.

So the following night one of my cousins slept in the same room with me. Neither of us saw or heard anything out of the way during that night or the early morning. That being the case, I persuaded myself that what I had seen had been only imagination, and much against everybody's expressed wish, I insisted the next night on sleeping in the room again, and alone. Accordingly, having retired again to the same room, I was kneeling down at the bedside to say my prayers, when exactly the same dread as before came over me. The curtains of the wardrobe swayed about, and I had the same sensation as previously, that I was not alone.

I felt too frightened to stir, when, luckily for me, one of my cousins came in for something which she had left. On looking at me she exclaimed, 'Have you seen anything?' I said 'No,' but told her how I felt, and, without much persuasion being necessary, I left the room with her, and never returned to it. When my hostess learnt what had happened (as she did immediately) she told me I must not sleep in that room again, as the nightmare had made such an impression on me; I should imagine (she said) all sorts of things and make myself quite ill. I went to another room, and during the rest of my visit (a week), I was not troubled by any reappearance of the little girl.

On leaving, my cousin, the eldest daughter of the doctor, went on a visit with me to the house of an uncle of mine in the same county. We stayed there for about a fortnight, and during that time the 'little girl' was alluded to only as my 'nightmare'.

In this I afterwards found there was a little reticence, for, just before leaving my uncle's, my cousin said to me, 'I must tell you something I have been longing to tell you ever since I left home. But my father desired me not to tell you, as, not being very strong, you might be too frightened. Your nightmare was not a nightmare at all, but the apparition of a little girl!' She then went on to tell me that this 'little girl' had been seen three times before, by three different members of the family; but as this was some nine or ten years since, they had almost ceased to think anything about it until I related my experiences on the morning after the first night of my second visit.

My cousin further went on to tell me that her younger sister whilst in bed had one morning, about daybreak, to her great surprise, seen a little girl with dark hair, standing with her back to her, looking out of the window. She took this figure for her little sister, and spoke to it. The child not replying, or moving from her position, she called out to it, 'It's no use standing like that; I know you. You can't play tricks with me.' On looking round, however, she saw that her little sister, the one she thought she was addressing and who was sleeping with her, had not moved from the bed.

Almost at the same time the child passed from the window into the room of her (my cousin's) sister A——, and the latter, as she afterwards declared, distinctly saw the figure of a child with dark hair standing by the side of a table in her room. She spoke to it, and it instantly disappeared. The 'little girl' was subsequently again seen, for the last time before I saw it, by my cousin's father, Dr H——. It was in the early daylight of a summer's morning, and he was going upstairs to his room, having just returned from a professional visit. On this occasion he saw the same child (he noticed its dark hair) running up the stairs immediately before him, until it reached his room and entered it. When he got into the room it was gone.

Thus the apparition has been seen three times by the family, and once by me. I am the only one, however, that has seen its face. It has, also, never been seen twice in the same room by anyone else.

*

We know very little about the witness of the second event from John Ingram's book except that he was a clergyman of the Church of England who told his story to a collector of ghostly apparitions, Robert Dale Owen.

THE STRANGE CASE OF THE LUMINOUS WOMAN

In the year 185– I was staying, with my wife and children, at a favourite watering-place. In order to attend to some affairs of my own, I determined to leave my family there for three or four days. Accordingly, one day in August, I took the railway and arrived in the evening, an unexpected guest, at —— Hall, the residence of a gentleman whose acquaintance I had recently made and with whom my sister was then staying.

I arrived late; soon afterwards went to bed, and before long fell asleep. Awaking after three or four hours, I was not surprised to find I could sleep no more; for I never rest well in a strange bed. After trying, therefore, in vain again to induce sleep, I began to arrange my plans for the day.

I had been engaged some little time in this way, when I became suddenly sensible that there was a light in the room. Turning round, I distinctly perceived a female figure; and what attracted my especial attention was, that *the light by which I saw it emanated from itself*. I watched the figure attentively. The features were not perceptible. After moving a little distance, it disappeared as suddenly as it had appeared.

My first thoughts were that there was some trick. I immediately got out of bed, struck a light, and found my bedroom door still locked. I then carefully examined the walls, to ascertain if there were any other concealed means of entrance or exit; but none could I find. I drew the curtains and opened the shutters; but all outside was silent and dark, there being no moonlight.

After examining the room well in every part, I betook myself to bed and thought calmly over the whole matter. The final impression on my mind was that I had seen something supernatural, and, if supernatural, that it was in some way connected with my wife. What was the appearance? What did it mean? Would it have appeared to me if I had been asleep instead of awake? These were questions very easy to ask and very difficult to answer.

Even if my room door had been unlocked, or if there had been a concealed entrance to the room, a practical joke was out of the question. For, in the first place, I was not on such intimate terms with my host as to warrant such a liberty; and, secondly, even if he had been inclined to sanction so questionable a proceeding, he was too unwell at the time to permit me for a moment to entertain such a supposition.

In doubt and uncertainty I passed the rest of the night; and in the morning, descending early, I immediately told my sister what had occurred, describing to her accurately everything connected with the appearance I had witnessed. She seemed much struck with what I told her, and replied, 'It is *very* odd; for you have heard, I dare say, that a lady was, some years ago, murdered in this house; but it was not in the room you slept in.' I answered that I had never heard anything of the kind, and was beginning to make further inquiries about the murder, when I was interrupted by the entrance of our host and hostess, and afterwards by breakfast.

After breakfast I left without having had any opportunity of renewing the conversation. But the whole affair had made upon me an impression which I sought in vain to shake off. The female figure was ever before my mind's eye, and I became fidgety and anxious about my wife. Could it in any way be connected with her? was my constantly recurring thought. So much did this weigh on my mind that, instead of attending to the business for the express purpose of transacting which I had left my family, I returned to them by the first train; and it was only when I saw my wife and children in good health, and everything safe and well in my household, that I felt satisfied that, whatever the nature of the appearance might have been, it was not connected with any evil to them.

On the Wednesday following I received a letter from my sister, in which she informed me that, since I left, she had ascertained that the murder *was* committed in the very room in which I had slept. She added that she purposed visiting us next day, and that she would like me to write out an account of what I had seen, together with a plan of the room, and that on that plan she wished me to mark the place of the appearance and of the disappearance of the figure.

This I immediately did; and the next day, when my sister arrived, she asked me if I had complied with her request. I replied, pointing to the drawing-room table, 'Yes; there is the account and the plan.' As she rose to examine it, I prevented her, saying, 'Do not look at it until you have told me all you have to say, because you might unintentionally colour your story by what you may read there.'

Thereupon she informed me that she had had the carpet taken up in the room I had occupied, and that the marks of blood from the murdered person were there, plainly visible, on a particular part of the floor. At my request she also then drew a plan of the room, and marked upon it the spots which still bore traces of blood.

The two plans – my sister's and mine – were then compared, and we verified the most remarkable fact, that *the places she had marked as the beginning and ending of the traces of blood, coincided exactly with the spots marked on my plan as those on which the female figure had appeared and disappeared.*

I am unable to add anything to this plain statement of facts. I cannot account in any way for what I saw. I am convinced no human being entered my chamber that night; yet I know that, being wide awake and in good health, I *did* distinctly see a female figure in my room. But if, as I must believe, it was a supernatural appearance, then I am unable to suggest any reason why it should have appeared to me. I cannot tell whether, if I had not been in the room, or had been asleep at the time, that figure would equally have been there. As it was, it seemed connected with no warning nor presage. No misfortune of any kind happened then, or since, to me or mine. It is true that the host, at whose house I was staying, when this incident occurred, and also one of his children, died a few months afterwards; but I cannot pretend to make out any connection between either of these deaths and the appearance I witnessed. . . . But what I distinctly saw, that, and that only, I describe.

3 The Gambling Ghosts

John Ingram's book is about ghosts in the great old houses and mansions of Britain. But, of course, ghosts do not live only in stately homes. They are also to be found in modern council houses and smart semi-detached suburban residences, as well as in factories and schools and prisons and ships: anywhere, in fact, that people spend their nights and days. Had Ingram talked to Scottish shepherds, for instance, he would have found a whole tribe of spirits lurking in crofts and cabins in the Highlands. This is one of the better known, recorded by a folklorist many years ago in the words of a Highland storyteller.

THE GHOSTS THE DOCTOR SAW

Away in the Highlands of Scotland some of the shepherds' houses are so isolated and far from the main road they are hard to reach. In fact, a lot of them has only a track to reach them, and in either mist or darkness is easy lost, and this accident happened many years ago.

A shepherd's wife turned ill, and it was at one of these isolated houses, far from the main road, and they had sent word for the doctor.

It was the short days of winter, and wet and misty weather prevailed; the doctor's way of travelling was on horseback, and it was mid-afternoon as he set out on his journey across the moors for the shepherd's house.

He had been there before, and he knew the track, but the mist and darkness came down, and he lost the track. He kept on trying to find it, till he was utterly lost. As he kept on wandering up and down, he saw a light through the mist and darkness, and he thought it must be a shepherd's house, and he made his way for it, as he thought they would be able to put him on the track. But before he reached the cottage the light went out, and when he reached it all was darkness. He thought they must have gone to bed, and he knocked at the door, but got no answer. So he went to the outhouse, and managed to get his horse into the byre, then he went back to the door, and, as he got no answer, he tried the door, and found it was not locked. So he went in; but to his great astonishment, the place was like as if no one had been in it for a long time, as the furniture was so dusty, and no signs of life. So he thought he would make the best of it for the night; and he managed to light a fire, and he had a bit lunch with him, he sat down at the fire and ate it. Then he had a look into what looked like the room end, where there was a bed, and a little table at the side of it. So, after sitting at the fire for some time, he rose and shut the outer door, and went ben into the room, and prepared to go to bed, as the night was so dark and misty he could not proceed any farther the night.

As he undressed he laid his purse and his gold watch on the little table, then went to bed. He was just beginning to dover over to sleep when he heard voices ben in the kitchen. They were men's voices, and they seemed to be arguing over something. He creeped over the bed, and very quietly keeked ben into the kitchen, and he was surprised to see two rough-looking men sitting at the table playing cards. There was a dispute about one of them cheating, and one had dropped a card, and as he stooped to pick it up, the other drew a long knife and stabbed him to death. The doctor got such a fright he crept back to bed, where he lay in terror. He kept well hidden under the clothes, and it was not long or the man came ben and looked round the room, and came up to the table at the bedside and lifted the doctor's watch and his purse of money. The doctor lay there sweating with fear, and lamenting the loss of his purse of money and his gold watch.

He lay for some time till he heard the man go out the door, but he lay listening in fear he would come back, till, overcome with sleep, he must have dovered away to sleep, and lay there till morning, and waked up, and his first thoughts were of the night before and the two men, and remembering his loss of his purse of money and gold watch. And it was his first thought – the two men and the murder. He thought of the murdered man lying on the floor, and he thought the sooner he was out of bed and out of this the better; so he jumped out of bed and was putting on his clothes, and, still thinking about his lost watch and purse, he happened to look down at the little table where he had laid his watch and money, when, to his great surprise, his gold watch and his purse were lying as he had left them the night before. He could hardly believe his own eyes, as he saw the murderer lift them the night before. He was not long in getting them into his pocket; and when he keeked ben into the kitchen he saw no man lying murdered on the floor, and everything was the same as when he left it the night before. He made for the byre to get his horse, as the mist had cleared away, and he now knew he could find his way. After getting his horse out, he rode off, and soon found the hill track to the shepherd's house. When he got there he told them of his experience last night.

After the shepherd thought awhile, he remembered

and told the doctor he had been in the drainers' haunted cottage, where the drainers lived, and one murdered his mate and fled the country, and was never heard of again, and the cottage has been haunted ever since.

4 Something Wicked This Way Comes

Just as some people are gifted footballers or tennis players or singers, there are people who seem to be gifted at seeing ghosts. We call them psychic. Some of these 'seers' decide to turn professional and use their gift as 'mediums', making their living from contacting ghosts. And that is when the trouble starts.

If a person claims to be a good tennis player, you can quite easily prove whether he is or is not. You watch him play. But mediums claim to be in touch with ghosts, and no matter how hard we try, no matter how much we might wish to, most of us cannot see ghosts, with the help of a medium or without. We have to take everything on trust; we cannot prove that the medium is what he claims to be. So it is easy for a confidence trickster to pretend to be a medium and to dupe the unwary. That is why many people are sceptical not just about ghosts but about mediums too.

On the other hand, there are undoubtedly people who quite genuinely believe they can 'get in touch' with ghosts, who seem to know when a ghost is present, and can even sometimes get rid of troublesome ones (to 'exorcise' them is the technical phrase) from their haunts.

Violet Tweedale claimed to be psychic. Her father was a ghost-seer too and used to take Violet with him on ghost-hunting expeditions when she was still a quite young child. For the rest of her life she encountered ghosts everywhere she went, and according to her book, *Ghosts I Have Seen*, she came into contact with some very strange spirits indeed.

One of the most frightening and certainly one of the most puzzling was an evil spirit that haunted a house in Torquay, the seaside town in Devon. Mrs Tweedale's involvement with it began quietly, but before long eight people in all were struggling with what she calls an 'emanation' of malicious character and criminal history.

Here is the story in her own words, an account quite as gripping as any tale invented by a writer of fiction.

THE TERRIFYING GHOST OF CASTEL A MARE
by Violet Tweedale

Some seven years ago, whilst wintering in Torquay, I heard a great deal of gossip about a villa on the Warberries, which was reputed to be badly haunted. For the last forty to fifty years nobody, it was said, had been able to live in it for any length of time. Several people asserted that they had heard screams coming from it as they passed along the high road, and no occupant had ever been able to keep a door shut or even locked.

The house is at present being pulled down, therefore I commit no indiscretion in describing the phenomena connected with it.

Castel a Mare is situated in what house agents would describe as 'a highly residential quarter'. It is surrounded by numerous villas, inhabited by people who are all very well-to-do, and who make Torquay their permanent home. The majority of these villas lie right back from the road, and are hidden in their own luxuriant gardens, but the haunted house is one of several whose back premises open straight on to the road.

No dwelling could have looked more commonplace or uninteresting. It was built in the form of a high box, three-storeyed. It was hideous and inartistic in the extreme, but along its frontage looking towards the sea and hidden from the road, there ran a wide balcony on to which the second-floor rooms opened, and from there the view over the garden was charming. When I first went to look at it, dilapidation had set in. Jackdaws and starlings were busy in the chimneys, the paint was peeling off the walls, and most of the windows were broken. Year after year those windows were mended, but they never remained intact for more than a week, and during the war there has been no attempt at renewal. Even the agents' boards, 'To be let or sold', dropped one by one from their stems, as if in sheer weariness of so fruitless an announcement.

It was not long before I obtained the loan of the keys, and proceeded to 'take the atmosphere'. It was decidedly unhealthy, I concluded, though I neither heard or saw anything unusual during the hour I spent alone in quietly wandering through the deserted rooms. I found no trace of tramps, and all the closed windows were thickly cobwebbed *inside*, an important fact to notice in psychic research. I fixed upon the bathroom and one other small room, as the *foci* of the trouble, and left the house with no other strong impression than that my movements had been closely watched, by someone unseen by me. It was no uncommon sight in pre-war days to see several smart motor cars drawn up at the gate. Frivolous parties of explorers in search of a thrill drove in from the surrounding neighbourhood, and romped gaily through the house and out again, and I discovered that several of those visitors had distinctly felt that they were being followed about and watched.

My husband and I were naturally much interested in this haunted dwelling, so accessible, and so near to our own house. We determined that if we could make friends with the owner we would do a little investigation on our own. Numerous people, on the plea that the house might suit them as a residence, got the loan of the keys, and spent an hour or two inside the place, wandering about the house and garden, but the owner was getting tired of this rush of spurious house-hunters. He was beginning to ask for *bona fides*, so we determined honestly to state our purpose.

The proprietor was an old builder who owned several other houses. He received me very civilly, even gratefully. He would willingly give us the keys for as long a period as we required them. Castel a Mare brought him extreme bad luck; he longed to be rid of it, and he added that if, after our investigations, my husband could give the house a clean bill of health it would be of enormous benefit to him, in enabling him to let or sell it. He did not seem very hopeful, but stated it to be his opinion that the hauntings were all nonsense, and that the screams people heard were the cries of some peacocks that lived in a property not far off. This sounded very reasonable, and I promised him that if we could honestly state that the house was perfectly healthy, we would permit our conclusions to be made public.

My husband and I decided that the hour from one p.m. till two p.m. would be the quietest and least conspicuous time in which to investigate. Doubtless the night would have been better still, but it would have created too much excitement in the neighbourhood, and callers to see how we were bearing up would have defeated our object. Between one and two all Torquay would be lunching, and we could easily slip in unobserved, and we would require neither lights nor warm comforts.

We started at once, my husband keeping the keys and making himself responsible for the doors. Though the window-panes were badly broken, there were no openings large enough to admit a small child, and, as I have said, the network of cobwebs within was evidence that no human being entered the house by the windows. The front door lock was in good order, and so were most of the other locks in the house. We shut ourselves in, and after a thorough examination of the premises we mounted to the first floor. Three rooms opened on to it, belonging to the principal bedroom – a smaller room and a bathroom opening out of the big bedroom. My husband closed all the doors, and we sat down on the lower steps of the bare staircase leading to the floor above. That day we drew an absolute blank, and at two o'clock we closed every door in the house, and just inside the front door we made a careless-looking arrangement of twigs, dead leaves, pieces of straw and dust, which could not fail to betray the passing of human feet, should anybody possess a duplicate key to the front door and enter by that means.

The second day we found our twig and straw arrangements intact, but not a single door was shut, all were thrown defiantly wide. This seemed rather promising and we went upstairs to our seat on the steps, and carefully reclosing the doors immediately in front of us, sat down to await events.

Quite half an hour must have passed when suddenly a click made us both look up. The handle of the door but a couple of yards distant from me, leading into the small room, was turning, and the door quietly opened wide enough to admit the passing of a human being. It was a bright sunny day, and one could see the brass knob turning round quite distinctly. We saw no form of any sort, and the door remained half open. For perhaps a couple of moments we awaited developments, then our attention was suddenly switched off the door by the sound of hurrying footsteps running along the bare boards on the corridor above us. My husband rushed up and searched each empty room, but neither saw anything nor heard anything more. Before leaving the house we shut all doors, and locked all that would lock. Such was the meagre extent of our second day's investigations.

On the third day the doors were all found wide flung. No door opened before our eyes as on our former visit, but a brushing sound was heard ascending the stairs, as if from someone pressing close against the wall.

For about a fortnight nothing happened beyond what I have recounted, but I was strongly conscious that we were being watched. The unhealthiest spots were the bathroom, a servants' room entered by a staircase leading from the kitchen, and the stable, a small building immediately to the right of the house. The bathroom was in great disrepair, long strips of paper hung from the walls, and an air of profound depression pervaded it. Obviously it had once been merely a large cupboard, and it had a window admitting light from a passage behind it.

We had never once failed to find every door which we had closed thrown wide on our return, and one day we locked the bathroom, and removing the key we looked about for some spot in which to secrete it. On that floor was nothing large enough to hide even so small an object as a key, so we took it downstairs to the dining room. In a corner lay a rag of linoleum about six inches square; under this we placed the bathroom key and left the house.

That afternoon a house agent called and asked for the loan of the keys. He told us that a brave widow lady, who knew the history of the house, thought it might suit her to live in, and he proposed to take her over it and point out its charms. He would return the keys to us directly afterwards. I took advantage of this occasion to say to the agent that probably the screams some people had heard proceeded from the peacocks in the neighbourhood.

He shook his head and answered, 'We hoped that might prove to be the case, but we have ascertained that it is not so.' He seemed despondent about the place, even though what we had to tell him was as yet nothing very formidable or exciting. What we did not tell him was that we had locked up the bathroom, and hidden the key. We left him to discover that fact for himself.

He returned with the keys in about an hour, and I asked him what the widow thought of Castel a Mare.

'She thinks something might be made of it. The cheapness attracts her,' he answered.

'But it will need so much doing to it,' I demurred. 'What did she think of the bathroom?'

'She said it only needed cleaning and repapering. The bath itself she found in good enough condition.'

So the bathroom door was open, in spite of our having locked it and hidden the key!

After the agent had gone we went to the house. Every door stood wide. The bathroom key was still in its hiding place, and the door open. We replaced the key. The ghosts laughed to scorn such securities as locks and keys.

For a month or two we pursued our investigations, then we returned the keys to the owner. Though we had seen and heard so little it was impossible to give the house a clean bill of health, and the old builder was much cast down. A few days afterwards we received a letter from him offering us the house as a free gift. It would pay him to be rid of the ground rent, and the place was as useless to him as to anyone else. We thanked him and refused the gift.

About this period I was lucky enough to get into touch with a former tenant of Castel a Mare, and this lady most kindly gave me many details of her residence there. About thirty years ago she occupied it with her father and mother, and they were the last family to live in it for any length of time, and for many years it has remained empty.

Soon after their arrival this family discovered that there was something very much amiss with their new residence. The house, the garden, and the stable were decidedly uncanny, but it was some time before they would admit, even to themselves, that the strange happenings were of a supernatural order.

The phenomena fell under three headings: a piercing scream heard continually, at any hour and during all seasons; continuous steps running along corridors, and up and down stairs; constant lockings of doors by unseen hands.

The scream was decidedly the most unnerving of the various phenomena. The family lived in constant dread of it. Sometimes it came from the garden, sometimes from inside the house. One morning whilst they sat at breakfast, they were violently startled by this horrible sound coming from the inner hall, just outside the room in which they sat. It took but a moment to throw open the door, but, as usual, there was nothing to be seen.

On another occasion the family doctor had just arrived at the front door, and was about to ring, when he was startled by the scream coming from inside the house. This doctor still lives in the neighbourhood, and is one of many people who can bear witness to the fact.

The footsteps of unseen people kept the family pretty busy. They were always running to the doors to see who was hurrying past, and up and down stairs. Very soon the drawing-room became extremely uncomfortable, and practically uninhabitable. It was always full of unseen people moving about. The lady of the house never felt herself alone, and when she found herself locked into her own room, the behaviour of her astral guests seemed to her to have become intolerable. The master of the house no more escaped these attentions than did the rest of the inhabitants, and finally all keys had to be removed from all doors.

One night some guests, after getting into bed, heard someone open the door of their room and enter. Astonishment kept them silent, and in a minute or two their visitor quietly withdrew and closed the door again. They concluded that it must have been their hostess, and that thinking they were asleep she had not spoken, yet still they thought the incident very strange. The next morning they discovered that no member of the household had entered their room.

On another occasion a lady who had come to help nurse a sick sister saw, one night, a strange woman dressed in black velvet walk downstairs.

Animals fared badly at Castel a Mare. A large dog belonging to the family was often found cowering and growling in abject fear of something visible to it, but not to the human inhabitants, and the harness horse showed such an invincible objection to its stable, that it could only be got in by backing.

Later on I was told that a member of the Psychical

Society had visited Castel a Mare and had pronounced the garden to be more haunted than the house.

In 1917 a friend rang me up and asked me if I would form one of a party of investigation at Castel a Mare. The services of a medium had been secured, and a soldier on leave, who was deeply immersed in psychic research, was in high hopes of getting some genuine results.

I accepted the invitation because a certain incident had once more roused my curiosity in the haunted house.

During our investigations I had been disappointed at not hearing the much-talked-of scream, the more so after learning from the former tenants how very often they had heard it. When I did at last hear it I was walking past the house on a very hot summer morning about eleven o'clock. I was not thinking of the house, and had just passed it on my way home, when a piercing scream arrested my attention. I wheeled round instantly; there was not a doubt as to where the scream came from, but unfortunately, though there were people on the road, there was no one near enough to bear witness. The scream appeared to come from someone in abject terror, and would have arrested the attention of any one who happened to be passing. I mean that had no haunted house stood there, had the scream proceeded from any other villa, I am sure that any passer-by would have halted wonderingly, and awaited further developments.

Castel a Mare lay in absolute silence, under the blazing sunshine, and in a minute or two I walked on. I could now understand what it must have meant to live in that house, in constant dread of that weird and hideous sound resounding through the rooms or garden.

This incident made me eager to join my friend's party, and on reaching the house I found a small crowd assembled.

The medium, myself, and four other women. The soldier, and an elderly and burly builder belonging to the neighbourhood, who was interested in psychic research. Eight persons in all.

As there was no chair or furniture of any description in the house, we carried in a small empty box from a rubbish heap outside, and followed the medium through the rooms. She elected to remain in the large bedroom on the first floor, out of which opened the bathroom, and she sat down on the box and leaned her back against the wall, whilst we lounged about the room and awaited events. It was a sunny summer afternoon, and the many broken panes of glass throughout the house admitted plenty of air.

After some minutes it was plain to see that the medium had fallen into a trance. Her eyes were closed, and she lay back as if in sound sleep. Time passed, nothing happened, we were all rather silent, as I had warned the party that though we were in a room at the side of the house farthest from the road, our voices could plainly be heard by passers-by, and we wanted no interference.

Just as we were all beginning to feel rather bored and tired of standing, the medium sprang to her feet with surprising agility, pouring out a volley of violent language. Her voice had taken on the deep growling tones of an infuriated man, who advanced menacingly towards those of us who were nearest to him. In a harsh, threatening voice he demanded to know what right we had to intrude on his privacy.

There was a general scattering of the scared party

before this unlooked-for attack, and the soldier gave it as his opinion that the medium was now controlled by the spirit of a very violent male entity. I had no doubt upon the point.

Then commenced so very unpleasant a scene that I had no doubt also of the medium's genuineness. No charlatan, dependent upon fraudulent mediumship for her daily bread, would have made herself so intensely obnoxious as did this frail little woman. I found myself saying, 'Never again. This isn't good enough.'

The entity that controlled her possessed superhuman strength. His voice was like the bellow of a bull, as he told us to be gone, or he would throw us out himself, and his language was shocking.

I had warned the medium on entering the house that we must be as quiet as possible, or we would have the police walking in on us. Now I expected any moment to see a policeman, or some male stranger arrive on the scene, and demand to know what was the matter.

The majority of our party were keeping at a safe distance, but suddenly the control rushed full tilt at the soldier, who had stood his ground, and attacking him with a tigerish fury drew blood at once. The big builder and I rushed forward to his aid. The rest of the party forsook us and fled pell-mell out of the house and into the garden. Glancing through a window, near which we fought, I saw below a row of scared faces staring up in awed wonder.

The scene being enacted was really amazing. This frail little creature threw us off like feathers, and drove us foot by foot before her, always heading us off the bathroom. We tried to stand our ground, and dodge her furious lunges, but she was too much for us. After a desperate scuffle, which lasted quite seven or eight minutes, and resulted in much torn clothing, she drove us out of the room and on to the landing. Then suddenly, without warning, the entity seemed to evacuate the body he had controlled, and the medium went down with a crash and lay at our feet, just a little crumpled, dishevelled heap.

For some considerable time I thought that she was dead. Her lips were blue, and I could feel no pulse. We had neither water nor brandy with which to revive her, and we decided to carry her down into the garden and see what fresh air would do. Though villas stood all round us, the foliage of the trees gave us absolute privacy, and we laid her flat on the lawn. There, after about ten minutes, she gradually regained her consciousness, and seemingly none the worse for her experiences she sat up and asked what had happened.

We did not give her the truth in its entirety, and contrived to account for the blood-stained soldier and the torn clothing, without unduly shocking and distressing her. We then dispersed; the medium walking off as if nothing whatever had occurred to deplete her strength.

Some days after this the soldier begged for another experiment with the medium. He had no doubts as to her genuineness, and he was sure that if we tried again we would get further developments. She was willing to try again, and so was the builder, but with one exception the rest of the party refused to have anything more to do with the unpleasant affair, and the one exception stipulated to remain in the garden. She very wisely remarked that if she came into the house there was no knowing what entity might not attach itself to her, and return home with her, and she was not going to risk it. Of course this real danger always has to be counted upon in such investigations, but as the men of the party desired a woman to accompany the medium, I consented, and we entered the house once more, a reduced party of four.

After the medium had remained entranced for some minutes, the same male entity again controlled her. The same violence, the same attacks began once more, but this time we were better prepared to defend ourselves. The soldier and the stalwart builder warded off the attacks, and tried conciliatory expostulations, but all to no purpose. Then the soldier, who seemed to have considerable experience in such matters, tried a system of exorcising, sternly bidding the malignant entity depart. There ensued a very curious spiritual conflict between the exorcist and the entity, in which sometimes it seemed as if one, then the other, was about to triumph.

Those wavering moments were useful in giving us breathing space from the assaults, and at length, having failed, as we desired, to get into the bathroom, we drove him back against the wall at the far end of the room. Finally the exorcist triumphed, and the medium collapsed on the floor, as the strength of the control left her.

For a few moments we allowed the crumpled-up little heap to remain where she lay, whilst we mopped our brows and regained our breath. The soldier had brought a flask of brandy which we proposed to administer to the unconscious medium, but quite suddenly a new development began.

She raised her head, and still crouching on the floor with closed eyes she began to cry bitterly. Wailing, and moaning, and uttering inarticulate words, she had become the picture of absolute woe.

'Another entity has got hold of her,' announced the

soldier. It certainly appeared to be so.

All signs of violence had gone. The medium had become a heart-broken woman.

We raised her to her feet, her condition was pitiable, but her words became more coherent.

'Poor master! On the bed. Help him! Help him!' she moaned, and pointed to one side of the room. Again and again she indicated, by clenching her hands on her throat, that death by strangulation was the culmination of some terrible tragedy that had been enacted in that room.

She wandered, in a desolate manner, about the floor, wringing her hands, the tears pouring down her cheeks, whilst she pointed to the bed, then towards the bathroom with shuddering horror.

Suddenly we were startled out of our compassionate sympathy by a piercing scream, and my thoughts flew instantly to the experiences of the former tenants, and what I myself had heard in passing on that June morning of the former year.

The medium had turned at bay, and began a frantic encounter with some entity unseen by us. Wildly she wrestled and fought, as if for her life, whilst she emitted piercing shrieks for help. We rushed to the rescue, dragging her away from her invisible assailant, but a disembodied fighter has a considerable pull over a fighter in the flesh, who possesses something tangible that can be seized. I placed the medium behind me, with her back to the wall, but though I pressed her close she continued to fight, and I had to defend myself as well as defend her. Her assailant was undoubtedly the first terrible entity which had controlled her. At intervals she gasped out, 'Terrible doctor – will kill me – he's killed master – help! help!'

Gradually she ceased to fight. The soldier was exorcising with all his force, and was gaining power; finally he triumphed, inasmuch as he banished the 'terrible doctor'.

The medium was, however, still under the control of the broken-hearted entity, and began again to wander about the room. We extracted from her further details. An approximate date of the tragedy. Her master's name, that he was mentally deficient when the murder took place. She was a maidservant in the house, and after witnessing the crime she appeared to have shared her master's fate, though by what means we could not determine. The doctor was a resident physician of foreign origin.

At last we induced her to enter the bathroom, which she seemed to dread, and there she fell to lamenting over the dead body of her master, which had lain hidden there when the room was used as a large cupboard. It was a very painful scene, which was ended abruptly by her falling down insensible.

She had collapsed in an awkward corner, but at last we lifted her out, and carried her downstairs to the garden. When I tried to revive her with brandy I found that her teeth were tightly clenched. I then tried artificial respiration, as I could feel no pulse. Gradually she came back to life, quietly, calmly, and in total ignorance of what had occurred. The most amazing thing was that she showed no signs whatever of exhaustion or mental fatigue. We were all dead beat, but not so the fragile-looking little medium, though externally she looked terribly dishevelled and draggled.

This was the last time I set foot in the haunted house, which is now being demolished, but I still had to experience more of its odd phenomena.

The date and names the medium had given us were

later on verified by means of a record of villa residenters, which for many years had been kept in the town of Torquay.

There is no one left now who has any interest in verifying a tragic story supposed to have been enacted about fifty years ago. It must be left in the realms of psychic research, by which means it was dragged to light. Certain it is that no such murder came to the knowledge of those who were alive then, and live still in Torquay.

If there is any truth in the story it falls under the category of undiscovered crimes. The murderer was able somehow to hide his iniquities and escape suspicion and punishment. I do not know if it is intended to build another house on the same site. I hope not, for it is very probable that a new residence would share the fate of the old. Bricks and mortar are no impediment to the free passage of the disembodied, and there is no reason why they should not elect to manifest for an indefinite period of time.

There can be no doubt that the scream was an actual fact. There are so many people living who heard it, and are willing to testify to the horror of it. Amongst those living people are former tenants, who for long bore the nervous strain of its constant recurrence.

There remains one other weird incident in connection with Castel a Mare which I will now try to describe.

In the winter of 1917 I was engaged in war work which took me out at night. Like every other coast town Torquay was plunged at sunset into deepest darkness, save when the moon defied the authorities. The road leading from the nearest tramcar to our house was not lit at all, and one had to stumble along as best one could, even electric torches being forbidden.

I was returning home one very dark, still night about a quarter past ten, and being very tired I was walking very slowly. Owing to the inky darkness I thought it best to walk in the middle of the road, in order to avoid the inequalities in the footpath at each garden entrance to the villas. At that hour there was no traffic, and not a soul about.

Suddenly my steps were arrested by a loud knocking on a window-pane, and I collected my thoughts and tried to take my bearings. The sound came from the left, where two or three villas stand close to the road. All I could distinguish was a denser blot of black against the dense surroundings, but by making certain calculations I recognised that I stood outside Castel a Mare. The knocking on the pane lasted only a moment or two, and was insistent and peremptory. I jumped to the instant conclusion that someone was having a lark inside, and was trying to get a rise out of me. I was too tired to be bothered, and moved on again with a strong inclination towards my own warm bed, when the knocking rang out more peremptorily than ever. It seemed to say 'Stop! don't go on. I have something to say to you.' Involuntarily I stood still again, and wished that some human being would pass along the road. I really would not have cared who it was, policeman, soldier, maidservant. I would have laid hold of them and said, 'Do you hear that knocking? It comes from the haunted house.'

Alas! no one did come. The night lay like an inky pall all about me, silent as the grave, save for that commanding order to stop which was rapped upon a window-pane whenever I attempted to move on.

Though the being who thus sought to detain me could not possibly distinguish who I was, or whether my gender was male or female, he could certainly hear my footsteps as I walked, and the cool inconsequence of his behaviour began to nettle me. I was about to move resolutely on when I heard something else. This time something really thrilling!

Peal after peal of light laughter, accompanied by flying feet. But such laughter! Thin, high treble laughter, right away up and out of the scale, and apparently proceeding from many persons. Such flying feet! racing, pattering, rushing feet, light as those of the trained athlete. I stood enthralled with wonder, for in the pitch-black darkness of that house surely no human feet could avoid disaster. They were rushing up and down that steep, bare wooden staircase that I knew so well, and the laughter and the swift-winged feet sounded now from the ground floor, then could be clearly traced ascending, till they reached the third and last floor. Tearing along the empty corridors, they began the breakneck descent again to the bottom, a pell-mell, wild rush of demented demons chasing each other. That is what it sounded like.

I must have stood there for quite ten minutes, longing intensely for someone to share in my experiences, but Torquay had gone to bed, and I felt it was time for me to do likewise.

What could I make of the affair? Nothing! Rats? Rats don't laugh. Human beings having a rag and trying to scare the neighbourhood? No human being could have run up and down that staircase in such profound darkness. It would have been a case of crawling up with a firm hand on the banister rail.

I gave up trying to think and turned resolutely away. As I did so the knocking began again upon the windowpane.

'Do stop; oh! don't go away. Stop! stop!' it seemed to call after me insistently as I quickened my footsteps and gradually outdistanced the imperious demand.

What explanations have I to offer? None! The hallucinations of a tired woman? That may do for the general public, but not for me. You see, I was the person who heard it.

5 A Ghost of the Future

One of the oddest things about ghosts is that they do not always have to belong to people or events from the past. There are an impressive number of reports about ghosts that turned out to belong to people still living, or even of ghosts that came from the future. Nobody has an entirely satisfactory explanation for these phenomena. All we can say for sure is that people who were in all other matters known to be honest have quite often recorded events for which there is no other explanation except that what they saw was some kind of ghost.

The following account is of a 'future ghost'. It first appeared in the society magazine, *The Tatler*. No author was named, the editor simply saying it was by 'a responsible person in good faith'.

THE PHANTOM COACH

The following experience was told me by the friend to whom it happened. He has to some extent the proverbial second sight of the Highland race, but takes it rather as a matter of course, and never speaks of these things. But on my pressing him on the subject of ghosts not long ago, he told me the following incident of his boyhood, which he said had often recurred to his mind as strange. It happened about twenty years ago, and I have withheld correct names.

His father owned a farm in the far north of Scotland, and when a boy of fourteen my friend set off one morning, with the shepherd's son and two dogs, to drive some sheep to the little market town of D——, some ten miles distant. They started at three a.m., just as the dawn was breaking. After a mile or so their road took a steep curve up the side of a mountain, with a drop of forty feet on one side. They had barely reached this curve when the dogs suddenly stopped still, gazing before them, and then, bristling with every sign of extreme terror, both began to howl. The sheep scattered up the hillside, and then an icy-cold wind blew past them, which my friend said seemed to go right through him.

Startled, he peered up the road in the pale morning light and saw a strange sight.

Galloping down out of the mist towards them came a coach and four, and the driver on the box was a lady in a dishevelled ball-dress, who was lashing at the horses and also seemed to be struggling to pull them up so as to round the curve. But at the pace they were going it was impossible. He heard the clatter and thunder of the terrified horses' hooves as the equipage tore past them, and he saw the woman's face clearly, as with a reckless yet desperate expression on it she wrestled with the horses, and in another second the poor beasts had plunged over the precipice with the heavy coach behind them. Instinctively he held his breath to listen for some sounds of the crash below, but none came. The normal silence reigned once more on the lonely road.

It had all happened in a few seconds, and as soon as the horror-struck lads could collect their senses they went to the edge of the road and peered over. There was nothing there! At the foot of the drop were only the usual shrubs and heather interpersed with rocks and entirely undisturbed.

The boys turned and looked at one another without a word. Then they silently collected the sheep and tramped the remaining miles of their journey, still without a single word to one another. Each boy was afraid that the other might not have seen what he had and would laugh at him as daft.

But when they arrived at the little town among acquaintances, they both burst out with the story of what they had seen. They corroborated one another in every detail, and both had recognised the lady, and named her. She was a certain Lady M—— of K——, well known in the Highlands; a woman of reckless and imperious nature, reputed to lead a somewhat fast and intemperate life.

The boys' tale consequently raised a great deal of excitement, gossip, and discussion; but on its being ascertained, through servants, that Lady M—— was in her own house at the time they were on the road, it dissolved into the belief that the tale was just a boyish hoax, and everyone simply refused to believe them.

Before many hours rumours had come to the ears of the minister, and after making inquiries, he very sharply rebuked my friend (whose father was a respected parishioner) for not only telling untruths, but taking the name of his elders and betters in vain. By the time the boys reached home again, being unable to account for the strange incident, they had set it aside for other, more everyday interests, as boys will.

Now comes the stranger sequel. That night Lady M—— of K—— attended a ball and started home in the early hours of the morning, driving her own coach and four, as she always insisted on doing. She was in an over-convivial and excited state of mind, and friends tried to dissuade her from such a proceeding over dangerous roads. But she was not in a mood to be argued with. She drove the horses down the steep hill at a mad pace, failed to take the curve, and they all went over the precipice at the exact spot where my friend had seen it happen. And from the time she was known to have left the ball, it must have been at almost the exact hour they saw it, but on the following morning. Lady M—— was found dead among the wreckage (which was really there this time) at the foot of the drop.

The news of this terrible accident was brought to the farm by the old minister, who apologised to the boys for his judgement of them. (Though it was rather a natural one after all!) But how can it be accounted for that a ghastly enactment of this tragedy should be rehearsed, as it were, exactly twenty-four hours before it took place in fact; and that the only witnesses of it should be two boys in no way connected with the lady concerned?

6   Witness to Murder

Australia sports the same kinds of ghosts as are to be found in Europe, and a few quite different ones nurtured by the Aboriginal inhabitants from the days before white settlers arrived, no doubt bringing with them their European spirits.

Of these original Australian spectres the best known is the flesh-curdling bunyip, a beast variously described as an amphibious animal, a gigantic snake, a sort of rhinoceros with a pulpy skin and a head like a calf's, and sometimes as a huge pig with a yellow body. Whatever it is, the bunyip is not pleasant.

Most famous of the late arrivals is the apparition of John Fisher. Australia's first home-grown fiction writer, John Lang, recorded the story in his book *Botany Bay, or True Stories of the Early Days of Australia*, published in 1859. (He meant, of course, the early days of the white man; the Aboriginals had lived there for hundreds if not thousands of years.) Many versions have appeared since then, but Lang's is the most interesting, because it captures the atmosphere and feeling of everyday life in Australia at the time when it was still a frontier land for the whites.

Lang was afraid that if he used the names of the real people involved he would be sued for libel, so he invented fictional names for them and set the story in Penrith instead of Campbelltown where it actually happened. It is a story as much about crime and murder as about ghosts and hauntings.

FISHER'S GHOST
by John Lang

It was a winter's night in the middle of July, when two wealthy farmers, in the district of Penrith, New South Wales, sat over the fire of a public house, which was about a mile distant from their homes. The name of the one was John Fisher, and of the other Edward Smith. Both of these farmers had been transported to the colony; had served their time; bought land; cultivated it; and prospered. Fisher had the reputation of being possessed of a considerable sum in ready money; and it was well known that he was the mortgagee of several houses in the town of Sydney, besides being the owner of a farm of three hundred acres, which was very productive, and on which he lived. Smith also was in good circumstances; arising out of his own exertions on his farm; but, unlike his neighbour, he had not put by much money.

'Why don't you go home, John, and see your friends and relations?' asked Smith. 'You be now very warm in the pocket; and, mark my words, they would be very glad to see you.'

'I don't know about that, friend,' replied Fisher. 'When I got into trouble, it was the breaking of the heart of my old father and mother; and none of my brothers and sisters – in all seven of 'em – have ever answered one of my letters.'

'You did not tell 'em you were a rich man, did you?'

'No; but I don't think they would heed that much, lad; for though they are far from wealthy, as small farmers, they are well-to-do in the world, and in a very respectable position in the country. I have often thought that if I was to go back, they would be sorry to see me, even if I carried with me a hundred thousand pounds.'

'Bless your innocent heart! You don't know human natur' as I do. Money does a deal – depend on't. Besides, who is to know anything about you, except your own family, and they would never go and hint that you had been unfortunate? How many years ago is it?'

'Let me see. I was then eighteen, and I am now forty-six – twenty-eight years ago. When I threw that stone at that man, I little thought it would hit him, much less kill him; and that I should be sent here for manslaughter. But so it was.'

'Why I recommend you, John, to go home is, because you are always talking of home and your relations. As for the farm, I'd manage that for you while you are away.'

'Thank you, Ned. I'll think about it.'

Presently the landlord entered the room, and Smith, addressing him, said, 'What think you, Mr Dean? Here is Mr Fisher going home to England to have a look at his friends and relations.'

'Is that true, Mr Fisher?' said the landlord.

'Oh, yes,' was Fisher's reply, after finishing his glass of punch, and knocking the ashes out of his pipe.

'And when do you think of going?' said the landlord.

'That'll depend,' replied Fisher, smiling. 'When I'm gone you will hear of it, not before; and neighbour Smith here, who is to manage the farm during my absence, will come and pay you any little score I may leave behind.'

'But I hope you will come and say goodbye,' said the landlord.

'Oh, of course,' said Fisher, laughing. 'If I don't, depend upon it you will know the reason why.'

The two farmers took their departure. Their farms adjoined each other, and they were always on the very best of terms.

About six weeks after the conversation above given, Smith called one morning at the public house, informed the landlord that Fisher had gone, and offered to pay any little sum that he owed. There was a small score against him; and while taking the money the landlord remarked that he was sorry Mr Fisher had not kept his word, and come to bid him goodbye. Mr Smith explained that Fisher had very good reasons for having his departure kept secret until after he had left the Colony; not that he wanted to defraud anybody, far from it, he added; and then darkly hinted that one of Mr Fisher's principal reasons for going off so stealthily was to prevent being annoyed by a woman who wanted him to marry her.

'Ah! I see,' said the landlord; 'and that's what he must have meant that night when he said, "If I don't, you'll hear the reason why." '

'I feel the loss of his society very much,' said Smith, 'for when we did not come here together to spend our evening, he would come to my house, or I would go to his, to play cards, smoke a pipe, and drink a glass of grog. Having taken charge of all his affairs, under a power of attorney, I have gone to live at his place, and left my overseer in charge of my own place. When he comes back, in the course of a couple of years, I am going home to England, and he will do for me what I am now doing for him. Between ourselves, Mr Dean, he has gone home to get a wife.'

'Indeed!' said the landlord. Here the conversation ended.

Fisher's sudden departure occasioned some surprise throughout the district; but when the explanation afforded by Mr Smith was spread abroad by Mr Dean, the landlord, people ceased to think about the matter.

A year elapsed, and Mr Smith gave out that he had received a letter from Fisher, in which he stated that it was not his intention to return to Sydney; and that he wished the whole of his property to be sold, and the proceeds remitted to him. This letter Mr Smith showed to several of Fisher's most intimate acquaintances, who regretted extremely that they would see no more of so good a neighbour and so worthy a man.

Acting on the power of attorney which he held, Mr Smith advertised the property for sale – the farm, the livestock, the farming implements, the furniture, etcetera, in the farmhouse – also some cottages and pieces of land in and near Sydney and Parramatta. With Fisher's mortgagors, also, he came to an agreement for the repayment, within a few months, of the sums due by them.

About a month previous to the day of sale, an old man, one David Weir, who farmed a small piece of land in the Penrith Road, and who took every week to the Sydney market, butter, eggs, fowls, and a few bushels of Indian maize, was returning to his home, when he saw, seated on a rail, the well-known form of Mr Fisher. It was very dark, but the figure and the face were as plainly visible as possible. The old man, who was not drunk, though he had been drinking at Dean's public house, pulled up, and called out, 'Halloa, Mr Fisher! I thought you were at home in England?' There was no reply, and the old man, who was impatient to get home, as was his horse, loosed the reins and proceeded on his journey.

'Mother,' said old Weir to his wife, while she was helping him off with his old topcoat, 'I've seen either Mr Fisher or his ghost.'

'Nonsense!' cried the old woman. 'You could not have seen Mr Fisher, for he is in Old England; and as for spirits, you never see any without drinking them; and you are full of 'em now.'

'Do you mean to say I'm drunk, mother?'

'No; but you have your liquor on board.'

'Yes; but I can see, and hear, and understand, and know what I am about.'

'Well, then, have your supper and go to bed; and take my advice, and say nothing to anybody about this ghost, or you will only get laughed at for your pains. Ghosts, indeed! at your age to take on about such things; after swearing all your life you never believed in them.'

'But I tell you I saw him as plain as plain could be; just as we used to see him sitting sometimes when the day was warm, and he had been round looking at his fences to see that they were all right.'

'Yes, very well; tell me all about it tomorrow,' said the old woman. 'As I was up before daylight, and it is now nearly midnight, I feel too tired to listen to a story about a ghost. Have you sold everything well?'

'Yes; and brought back all the money safe. Here it is.' The old man handed the bag over to his partner, and retired to his bed; not to rest, however, for the vision had made so great an impression upon his mind he could not help thinking of it, and lay awake till daylight, when he arose, as did his wife, to go through the ordinary avocations of the day. After he had milked the cows, and brought the filled pails into the dairy, where the old woman was churning, she said to him:

'Well, David, what about the ghost?'

'I tell you I seed it,' said the old man. 'And there's no call for you to laugh at me. If Mr Fisher be not gone away – and I don't think he would have done so without coming to say goodbye to us – I'll make a talk of this. I'll go and tell Sir John, and Doctor Mackenzie, and Mr Cox, and old Parson Fulton, and everybody else in the commission of the peace. I will, as I'm a living man! What should take Fisher to England? England would be no home for him after being so many years in this country. And, what's more, he has told me as much many a time.'

'Well, and so he has told me, David. But then, you know, people will alter their minds, and you heard what Mr Smith said about that woman?'

'Yes. But I don't believe Smith. I never had a good opinion of that man, for he could never look me straight in the face, and he is too oily a character to please me. If, as I tell you, Mr Fisher is not alive in this country, then that was his ghost that I saw, and he has been murdered!'

'Be careful, David, what you say; and whatever you do, don't offend Mr Smith. Remember, he is a rich man, and you are a poor one; and if you say a word to his discredit, he may take the law of you, and make you pay for it; and that would be a pretty business for people who are striving to lay by just enough to keep them when they are no longer able to work.'

'There's been foul play, I tell you, old woman. I am certain of it.'

'But that can't be proved by your saying that you saw

a ghost sitting on a rail, when you were coming home from market none the better for what you drank upon the road. And if Mr Fisher should be still alive in England – and you know that letters have been lately received from him – what a precious fool you would look!'

'Well, perhaps you are right. But when I tell you that I saw either Mr Fisher or his ghost sitting on that rail, don't laugh at me, because you will make me angry.'

'Well, I won't laugh at you, though it must have been your fancy, old man. Whereabouts was it you saw, or thought you saw him?'

'You know the cross-fence that divides Fisher's land from Smith's – near the old bridge, at the bottom of Iron Gang Hill?'

'Yes.'

'Well, it was there; I'll tell you what he was dressed in. You know that old fustian coat, with the brass buttons, and the corduroy waistcoat and trousers, and that red silk bandanna handkerchief that he used to tie round his neck?'

'Yes.'

'Well, that's how he was dressed. His straw hat he held in his left hand, and his right arm was resting on one of the posts. I was about ten or eleven yards from him, for the road is broad just there, and the fence stands well back.'

'And you called him, you say?'

'Yes; but he did not answer. If the horse had not been so fidgety, I'd have got down and gone up to him.'

'And then you would have found out that it was all smoke.'

'Say that again, and you will put me into a passion.'

The old woman held her tongue, and suffered old David to talk all that day and the next about the ghost, without making any remark whatever.

On the following Wednesday – Thursday being the market day in Sydney – old David Weir loaded his cart, and made his way to the Australian metropolis. True to his word with his wife, he did not mention to a soul one syllable touching the ghost. Having disposed of his butter, eggs, poultry and maize, the old man left Sydney at four o'clock, and, at half-past ten, arrived at Dean's public house.

He had travelled in that space of time thirty miles, and was now about eight or nine from home. As was his wont, he here baited the horse; but declined taking any refreshment himself, though pressed to do so by several travellers who wanted to 'treat' him. During the whole day he had been remarkably abstemious.

At a quarter to twelve the old man reharnessed his jaded horse, and was about to resume his journey, when two men, who were going to Penrith, asked him for a lift.

'Jump up, my lads,' said old David; and off they were driven at a brisk walk. One of the men in the cart was a ticket-of-leave man, in the employ of Mr Cox, and had been to Sydney to attend muster. The other was a newly appointed constable of the district. Both of these men had lived for several years in the vicinity of Penrith, and knew by sight all the inhabitants, male and female, free and bond.

When they neared the spot where the old man had seen the apparition, he walked the horse as slowly as possible, and again beheld the figure of Mr Fisher, seated on the upper rail of the fence, and in precisely the same attitude and the same dress.

'Look there!' said old David to the two men. 'What is that?'

'It is a man!' they both replied. 'But how odd! It seems as if a light were shining through him!'

'Yes,' said old David; 'but look at him. What man is it?'

'It is Mr Fisher,' they said, simultaneously.

'Hold the reins, one of you,' said old David. 'I'll go and speak to him. They say he is at home in England; but I don't believe it.'

Descending from the cart, the old man, who was as brave as a lion, approached the spectre, and stood within a few feet of it. 'Speak!' he cried. 'Don't you know me, sir? I am David Weir. How came you by that gash in your forehead? Are you alive or dead, Mr Fisher?' To these questions no answer was returned. The old man then stretched forth his hand and placed it on what appeared to be Mr Fisher's shoulder; but it was only empty air, vacant space, that the intended touch rested upon!

'There has been foul play!' said the old man, addressing the spectre, but speaking sufficiently loud to be heard by both men in the cart. 'And, by heaven, it shall be brought to light! Let me mark the spot.' And with these words he broke off several boughs from a tree near the rail, and placed them opposite to where the spectre remained sitting. Nay, further, he took out his clasp knife, and notched the very part on which the right hand of the spectre rested.

Even after the old man returned to the cart, the apparition of Mr Fisher, exactly as he was in the flesh, was 'palpable to the sight' of all three men. They sat gazing at if for full ten minutes, and then drove on in awe and wonderment.

When old David Weir arrived home, his wife, who was delighted to see him so calm and collected, inquired, laughingly, if he had seen the ghost again. 'Never mind about that,' said the old man. 'Here take the money, and lock it up, while I take the horse out of the cart. He is very tired, and no wonder, for the roads are nearly a foot deep in dust. This is the fifteenth month that has passed since we had the last shower of rain; but never mind! If it holds off for a fortnight or three weeks longer, our maize will be worth thirty shillings a bushel. It is wrong to grumble at the ways of Providence. In my belief it is very wicked.'

'Well, I think so, too,' said the old woman. 'Thirty shilling a bushel! Why, Lord a bless us, that'll set us up in the world, surely! What a mercy we did not sell when it rose to nine and sixpence!'

'Get me some supper ready, for as soon as I have taken it, I have some business to transact.'

'Not out of the house?'

'Never you mind. Do as I tell you.'

Having eaten his supper, the old man rose from his chair, put on his hat, and left his abode. In reply to his wife's question, 'Where are you going?' he said, 'To Mr Cox's; I'll be home in an hour or so. I have business, as I told you, to transact.'

The old woman suggested that he could surely wait till the morning; but he took no heed of her, and walked away.

Mr Cox was a gentleman of very large property in the district, and was one of the most zealous and active magistrates in the Colony. At all times of the day or the night he was accessible to any person who considered they had business with him.

It was past two o'clock in the morning when David Weir arrived at Mr Cox's house, and informed the watchman that he desired to see the master. It was not the first time that the old man had visited Mr Cox at such an hour. Two years previously he had been plundered by bushrangers, and, as soon as they had gone, he went to give the information.

Mr Cox came out, received the old man very graciously, and invited him to enter the house. Old David followed the magistrate, and detailed all that the reader is in possession of touching the ghost of Mr Fisher.

'And who were with you,' said Mr Cox, 'on the second occasion of your seeing this ghost?'

'One is a ticket-of-leave man, named Williams, a man in your own employ; and the other was a man named Hamilton, who lived for several years with Sir John Jamieson. They both rode with me in my cart,' was the old man's answer.

'Has Williams returned?'

'Yes, sir.'

'It is very late, and the man may be tired and have gone to bed; but, nevertheless, I will send for him.' And Mr Cox gave the order for Williams to be summoned.

Williams in a few minutes came, and corroborated David Weir's statement in every particular.

'It is the most extraordinary thing I ever heard in my life,' said Mr Cox. 'But go home, Weir, and you, Williams, go to your rest. Tomorrow morning I will go with you to the spot and examine it. You say that you have marked it, Weir?'

'Yes, sir.'

The old man then left Mr Cox, and Williams returned

to his hut. Mr Cox did not sleep again till a few minutes before the day dawned, and then, when he dropped off for a quarter of an hour, he dreamt of nothing but the ghost sitting on the rail.

The next morning, or rather on that morning, Mr Cox, at eight o'clock, rode over to the township of Penrith, and saw Hamilton, Weir's second witness. Hamilton, as did Williams, corroborated all that Weir had stated, so far as related to the second time the spectre had been seen; and Hamilton further volunteered the assertion that no one of the party was in the slightest degree affected by drink.

There was a tribe of blacks in the vicinity, and Mr Cox sent for the chief and several others. The European name of this chief was 'Johnny Crook', and, like all his race, he was an adept in tracking. Accompanied by Weir, Hamilton, Williams, and the blacks, Mr Cox proceeded to the spot. Weir had no difficulty in pointing out the exact rail. The broken boughs and the notches on the post were his unerring guides.

Johnny Crook, after examining the rail very minutely, pointed to some stains, and exclaimed, 'White man's blood!' Then, leaping over the fence, he examined the brushwood and the ground adjacent. Ere long he started off, beckoning Mr Cox and his attendants to follow. For more than three-quarters of a mile, over forest land, the savage tracked the footsteps of a man, and something trailed along the earth (fortunately, so far as the ends of justice were concerned, no rain had fallen during the period alluded to by Old David, namely, fifteeen months. One heavy shower would have obliterated all these tracks, most probably; and, curious enough, that very night there was a frightful downfall, such a downfall as had not been known for many a year), until they came to a pond, or waterhole, upon the surface of which was a bluish scum. This scum the blacks, after an examination of it, declared to be 'white man's fat'.

The pond in question was not on Fisher's land, or Smith's. It was on Crown land, in the rear of their properties. When full to the brink, the depth of the water was about ten feet in the centre; but at the time referred to there was not more than three feet and a half, and badly as the cattle wanted water, it was very evident, from the absence of recent hock-prints, that they would not drink at this pond. The blacks walked into the water at the request of Mr Cox, and felt about the muddy bottom with their feet. They were not long employed thus, when they came upon a bag of bones, or, rather, the remains of a human body, kept together by clothing, which had become so rotten it would scarcely bear the touch. The skull was still attached to the body, which the blacks raised to the surface and brought on shore, together with a big stone, and the remains of a large silk handkerchief. The features were not recognisable, but the buttons on the clothes, and the boots were those which Mr Fisher used to wear! And in the pocket of the trousers was found a buckhorn-handled knife, which bore the initials J.F., engraved on a small silver plate. This was also identified by Weir, who had seen Mr Fisher use the knife scores of times. It was of those knives which contained a large blade, two small ones, a corkscrew, gimlet, horse-shoe picker, tweezers, screwdriver, etcetera. The murderer, whoever it might be, had either forgotten to take away this knife, or had purposely left it with the body, for all the other pockets were turned inside out.

'Well, sir, what do you think of that?' said old Weir

to Mr Cox, who looked on in a state of amazement which almost amounted to bewilderment.

'I scarcely know what to think of it,' was Mr Cox's reply. 'But it is lucky for you, David, that you are a man of such good character that you are beyond the pale of being suspected of so foul a deed.'

'I, sir?'

'Yes, you. If it were not that this dead man's property is advertised for sale, it might have gone very hard with you, old man. It would have been suggested that your conscience had something to do with the information you gave me of the ghost. But stay here, all of you, with the body until I return. I shall not be absent for more than an hour. Have you a pair of handcuffs about you, Hamilton?'

'Several pairs, sir,' replied the constable.

After leaving the dead body, Mr Cox rode to Fisher's house, in which Mr Smith was living. Mr Smith, on being informed of the approach of so exalted a person as Mr Cox, one of the proudest men in the Colony, came out to receive him with all respect and honour. Mr Cox – who would not have given his hand to an 'expiree' (under any circumstances), no matter how wealthy he might be – answered Mr Smith's greeting with a bow, and then asked if he could speak with him for a few minutes. Mr Smith replied, 'Most certainly, sir;' and ordering a servant to take the magistrate's horse to the stables, he conducted his visitor into the best room of the weather-boarded and comfortable tenement. The furniture was plain and homely, but comfortable, nevertheless, and remarkably clean. The pictures on the walls formed rather a motley collection, having been picked up at various times by Mr Fisher at sales by public auction of the effects of deceased officials. Amongst others were two valuable oil-paintings, which had originally belonged to Major Ovens, an eccentric officer, who was buried on Garden Island, in the harbour of Port Jackson. These had been bought for less money than the frames were worth. There were also some Dutch paintings, of which neither Mr Fisher nor those who had not bid against him little knew the real value when they were knocked down for forty-two shillings the set – six in number!

'I have come to speak to you on a matter of business,' said the magistrate. 'Is the sale of this farm and the stock to be a peremptory sale? That is to say, will it be knocked down, bona fide, to the highest bidder?'

'Yes, sir.'

'And the terms are cash?'

'Yes, sir.'

'Sales for cash are not very common in this country. The terms are usually ten per cent deposit, and the residue at three, six, nine, and twelve months, in equal payments.'

'Very true, sir; but these are Mr Fisher's instructions, by which I must be guided.'

'What do you imagine the farm will realise, including the stock and all that is upon it?'

'Well, sir, it ought to fetch fifteen hundred pounds ready money.'

'I hear that the whole of Mr Fisher's property is to be sold, either by auction or private contract?'

'Yes, sir.'

'What will it realise, think you, in cash?'

'Not under twelve thousand pounds, I should say, sir.'

'One of my brothers has an idea of bidding for this farm: what about the title?'

'As good as can be, sir. It was originally granted to Colonel Foucaux, who sold it and conveyed it to Mr Thomas Blaxsell, who sold it and conveyed it to Fisher. But, as you know, sir, twenty years' undisputed possession of itself makes a good title, and Fisher has been on this farm far longer than that. All the deeds are here; you may see them, if you please, sir.'

'There is no occasion for that; as Mr Fisher's constituted attorney, you will sign the deed of conveyance on his behalf.'

'Yes, sir.'

'What is the date of the power of attorney?'

'I will tell you, sir, in one moment;' and, opening a bureau which stood in one corner of the room, Mr Smith produced the deed, and placed it in Mr Cox's hands.

With the signature of Fisher, Mr Cox was not acquainted; or, at all events, he could not swear to it. He had seen it – seen Fisher write his name, it is true; but, then, it was that sort of hand which all uneducated and outdoor working-men employ when they write their names – a sprawling round hand. But as to the signatures of the attesting witnesses, there could be no question whatever. They were those of two of the most eminent solicitors (partners) in Sydney – Mr Cox's own solicitors, in fact.

'And the letter of instructions, authorising you to sell by auction, for cash; for it says in this power, "and to sell the same, or any part thereof, in accordance with such instructions as he may receive from me by letter after my arrival in England."'

'Here is the letter, sir,' said Mr Smith, producing it.

Mr Cox read the letter attentively. It ran thus:

Dear Sir, I got home all right, and found my friends and relations quite well and hearty, and very glad to see me again. I am so happy among 'em, I shan't go out no more to the Colony. So sell all off, by public auction, or by private contract, but let it be for cash, as I want the money sharp; I am going to buy a share in a brewery with it. I reckon it ought, altogether, to fetch about £17,000. But do your best, and let me have it quick, whatever it is.

Your faithful friend,

JOHN FISHER

There was no postmark on this letter. In those days the postage on letters was very high, and nothing was more common for persons in all conditions of life to forward communications by private hand. As to the signature of the letter, it was identical with that of the power of attorney.

'All this is very satisfactory,' said Mr Cox. 'Is this letter, dated five months ago, the last you have received?'

'Yes, sir. It came by the last ship, and there has not been another in since.'

'Good morning, Mr Smith.'

'Good morning, sir.'

Riding away from Fisher's late abode, Mr Cox was somewhat perplexed. That power of attorney, drawn up so formally, and signed by Fisher in the presence of such credible witnesses, and then the letter written, signed in the same way by the same hand, were all in favour of the presumption that Fisher had gone to England, leaving his friend and neighbour Smith in charge of his property, real and personal. But then, there were the remains! And that they were the remains of Fisher, Mr Cox firmly believed. When he had returned to the pond, by a circuitous route, Mr Cox ordered the blacks to strip from a blue gum tree, with their tomahawks, a large sheet of bark. Upon this the remains were placed, carried straightway to Fisher's house (Mr Cox, upon horseback, heading the party), and placed in the verandah. While this proceeding was in progress, Mr Smith came out, and wore upon his countenance an expression of surprise, astonishment, wonder. But there was nothing in that. The most innocent man in the world would be surprised, astonished, and in wonderment on beholding such a spectacle.

'What is this, Mr Cox?' he said.

'The last that I have heard and seen of Mr Fisher,' was the reply.

'Of Mr Fisher, sir!'

'Yes.'

'There were his old clothes,' said Mr Smith, examining them carefully, 'most certainly this was the old suit he used to wear. But as for the body, it can't be his; for he is alive, as you have seen by his letter. These old clothes he must have given away, as he did many other old things, the day before he left this; and the man to whom he gave 'em must have been murdered.'

'Do you think he could have given away this knife?' said David Weir. 'To my knowledge, he had it for better than twelve years, and often have I heard him say he would not part with it for fifty pounds.'

'Give it away? Yes!' said Smith. 'Didn't he give away his old saddle and bridle? Didn't he give away his old spurs? Didn't he give away a cow and a calf?'

'He was a good man, an honest man, a very fair-dealing man, and in his latter days a very righteous and godly man; but he was not a giving-away man by any manner of means,' returned old David.

'And if he gave away these boots,' said Hamilton, 'they were a very good fit for the man who received them.'

'This man, whoever he is, was murdered, no doubt,' said Mr Smith, with the most imperturbable countenance and the coolest manner. 'Just look at this crack in his skull, Mr Cox.'

'Yes, I have seen that,' said the magistrate.

'And that's where poor Fisher's ghost had it,' said old David.

'Fisher's ghost!' said Mr Smith. 'What do you mean, Weir?'

'Why, the ghost that I have seen sitting on the rail not far from the old bridge at the bottom of the hill yonder.'

'Ghost! you have seen a ghost, have you?' returned Mr Smith, giving Mr Cox a very cunning and expressive look. 'Well, I have heard that ghosts do visit those who have sent them out of this world, and I dare say Mr Cox has heard the same. Now, if I had been you, I'd have held my tongue about a ghost (for ghosts are only the creatures of our conscience) for fear of being taken in charge.'

'I taken in charge!' said old Weir. 'No, no! my conscience is clear, and what I have seen and said I'll swear to. Wherever I go, I'll talk about it up to my dying hour. That was the ghost of Mr Fisher that I saw, and these are the remains of his body.'

'If I were Mr Cox, a magistrate,' said Mr Smith, 'I would give you in charge.'

'I will not do that, Mr Smith,' replied Mr Cox. 'I feel that my duty compels me to give you in custody of this police officer.'

'For what, sir?'

'On a charge of wilful murder. Hamilton!'

'Yes, sir.'

'Manacle Mr Smith, and take him to Penrith.'

Mr Smith held up his wrists with the air of an injured and pure-minded man, who was so satisfied of his innocence that he was prepared for the strictest investigation into his conduct, and had no dread as to the result.

A coroner's inquest was held on the remains found in the pond and a verdict of 'Wilful Murder' was returned against Edward Smith. The jury also found that the remains were those of John Fisher, albeit, they were so frightfully decomposed that personal identification was out of all question.

The vessel in which Fisher was reported to have left Sydney happened to be in the harbour. The captain and officers were interrogated, and in reply to the question – 'Did a man named John Fisher go home in your vessel?' – the reply was, 'Yes, and on the Customhouse officers coming on board, as usual, to look at the passengers and search the ship, to see that no convicts were attempting to make their escape, he produced his parchment certificate of freedom, in which there was a description of his person.'

'And did the man answer exactly to that description?'

'Yes, making allowance for his years, on looking at the date of the certificate. If he had not, he would have been detained, as many convicts have been.'

'And, during the voyage, did he talk of himself?'

'Frequently; he said that he was a farmer near Penrith; that, after he had served his time, he went to work, earned some money, rented a farm, then bought it, and by industry and perseverance had made a fortune.'

'Did he ever mention a Mr Smith – a friend of his?'

'Often. He said he had left everything in Mr Smith's hands, and that he did not like to sell his property till he saw how he should like England after so long an absence. He further said that if he did not come back to the Colony, he would have all his property sold off, and join some trading firm in his own country.'

The solicitor who had prepared the power of attorney, and witnessed it, said that a person representing himself as John Fisher of Ruskdale, in the district of Penrith, came to them and gave instructions for the deed; and, after it was duly executed, took it away with him, and requested that a copy might be made and kept in their office, which was done accordingly. In payment of the bill, twenty dollars (£5 currency), he gave a cheque on the Bank of New South Wales, which was cashed on presentation; that the man who so represented himself as John Fisher was a man of about forty-six or forty-eight years of age, about five feet eight inches in height, and rather stout; had light-blue eyes, sandy hair, and whiskers partially grey, a low but intelligent forehead, and a rather reddish nose.

This description answered exactly that of Mr Fisher at the time of his departure from the Colony.

The cashier of the bank showed the cheque for twenty dollars. Mr Fisher had an account there, and drew out his balance, £200 (not in person, but by a cheque), two days previous to his alleged departure. He had written several letters to the bank, and on comparing those letters with the letter Mr Smith said he had received from England, they corresponded exactly.

Opinion was very much divided in the Colony with respect to Mr Smith's guilt. Numbers of persons who knew the man, and had dealings with him, thought him incapable of committing such a crime, or any heinous offence, in fact. The records were looked into, to ascertain of what offence he had been convicted originally. It was for embezzling the sum of twenty-two shillings and fourpence, which had been entrusted to him when he was an apprentice for his master, who was a market gardener, seedsman, and florist. As for the story about the ghost, very, very few put any trust in it. Bulwer was then a very young gentleman, and had never dreamt of writing about Eugene Aram; nor had Thomas Hood contemplated his exquisite little poem on the same subject. Nor had the murder of the Red Barn been brought to light through the agency of a dream. The only instance of ghosts coming to give evidence of murder were those of Banquo and Hamlet's father; and Shakespeare was not considered an authority to be relied upon in such a case as that of Fisher.

Smith's house and premises, as well as those of Fisher, were searched in the hope of finding apparel, or some garment stained with blood, but in vain. Nor did the inspection of Smith's letters and papers disclose aught that strengthened the case against him. On the contrary, his accounts touching Fisher's property were kept entirely distinct from his own, and in memorandum books were found entries of the following description:

9 Sept. Wrote to Fisher to say P. has paid the interest on his mortgage.

27 Sept. Received £27/10/- from Wilson for year's rent of Fisher's house in Castlereagh Street.

12 Nov. Paid Baxter £3/12/- due to him by Fisher for bullock chains.

No case had ever before created, and probably never will again create, so great a sensation. Very many were firmly impressed with the belief that Weir was the murderer of the man who wore Fisher's clothes, crediting Smith's assertion or suggestion that he had given them away. Many others were of the opinion that the remains were those of Fisher, and the man who murdered him had robbed him of his certificate of freedom, as well as of the cash and papers he had about him, and then, representing Fisher, had got out of the Colony, and made Smith a dupe.

The anxiously looked-for day of trial came. The court was crowded with persons in every grade of society, from the highest to the very lowest. Mr Smith stood in the dock as firmly and as composedly as though he had been arraigned for a mere libel, or a common assault – the penalty not exceeding a fine and a few months' imprisonment.

The case was opened by the Attorney General with the greatest fairness imaginable, and when the witnesses gave their evidence (Weir, Hamilton and Mr Cox), everyone appeared to hold his breath. Smith, who defended himself, cross-examined them all with wonderful tact and ability; and, at the conclusion of the case for the prosecution, addressed the jury at considerable length, and with no mean amount of eloquence.

The judge then summed up. His Honour was the last man in the world to believe in supernatural appearances; but, with the ability and fairness that characterised his career in the Colony, he weighed the probabilities and improbabilities with the greatest nicety. To detail all the points taken by the judge would be tedious; but if his charge had any leaning one way or other, it was in favour of the prisoner.

The jury in those days was not composed of the

people, but of military officers belonging to the regiment quartered in the Colony. These gentlemen, in ordinary cases, did not give much of their minds to the point at issue. Some of them usually threw themselves back, and shut their eyes – not to think, but 'nod'. Others whispered to each other, not about the guilt or innocence of the prisoner at the bar, but about their own affairs; whilst those who had any talent for drawing, exercised it by sketching the scene, or taking the likeness of the prisoner, the witnesses, the counsel, the sheriff, and the judge. But in this case they seemingly devoted all their energies, in order to enable them to arrive at the truth. To every word that fell from the judge during his charge, which lasted over two hours, they listened with breathless attention, and when it was concluded, they requested permission to retire to consider their verdict. This was at half-past five in the afternoon of Friday, and not until a quarter to eleven did the jury return into court, and retake their places in the box.

The excitement that prevailed was intense, and when the murmurs in the crowd, so common upon such occasions, had subsided, amidst awful stillness the prothonotary put that all-momentous question, 'Gentlemen of the jury, what say you? Is the prisoner at the bar guilty, or not guilty?'

With a firm, clear voice, the foreman, a captain in the army, uttered the word – 'Guilty!'

Murmurs of applause from some, and of disapprobation from others, instantly resounded through the hall of justice. From the reluctant manner in which the judge put the black cap upon his head, it was evident that he was not altogether satisfied with the finding of the jury. He had, however, no alternative; and in the usual formal manner, he sentenced the prisoner to be hanged on the following Monday morning, at eight o'clock.

Smith heard the sentence without moving a single muscle, or betraying any species of emotion, and left the dock with as firm a step as that which he employed when entering it. His demeanour throughout the trial, and after he was sentenced, brought over many who previously thought him guilty to a belief in his innocence, and a petition to the Governor to spare his life was speedily drafted and numerously signed. It was rumoured that the Chief Justice, who tried the case, had also made a similar recommendation, and that the Governor, in deference thereto, had ordered a reprieve to be made out; but not to be delivered to the sheriff until seven o'clock on Monday morning. It was further stated that the Governor was of opinion that the finding of the jury was a correct one. The Press of the Colony did not lead, but fell into, the most popular opinion, that it would be tantamount to murder to take away the life of any human being upon such evidence as that given on the trial.

On the Monday morning, so early as half past six, the rocks which overlooked the gaol-yard in Sydney, and commanded a good view of the gallows, were crowded with persons of the lower orders; and when, at a little before seven, the hangman came out to suspend the rope to the beam, and make other preparations, he was hailed with loud hisses and execrations: so emphatic was the demonstration of the multitude in favour of the condemned man. By seven o'clock the mob was doubled; and when the under-sheriff or any other functionary was seen in the courtyard, the yells with which he was greeted were something terrific.

At five minutes to eight, the culprit was led forth, and at the foot of the gallows, and near his coffin (according to the custom prevailing in the Colony), was pinioned, preparatory to ascending the ladder. Whilst this ceremony was being performed, the shouts of the populace were deafening. 'Shame! Shame! Shame! Hang Weir! He is the guilty man! This is a murder. A horrid murder!' Such were the ejaculations that resounded from every quarter of that dense mob assembled to witness the execution; while the calm and submissive manner in which Smith listened to the reverend gentleman, who attended him in his last moments, heightened rather than suppressed the popular clamour.

At one minute past eight the fatal bolt was drawn, and Smith, after struggling for about half a minute, was dead! Whereupon the mob renewed their yells, execrations, hisses, and cries of 'Shame! Shame! Shame! Murder! Murder! Murder!' These noises could not recall to life Mr Smith. He had gone to his account, and after hanging an hour, his body was cut down; the coffin containing it conveyed, in an uncovered cart, to Slaughter-House Point (the last resting place of all great criminals), and the grave filled in with quicklime.

There was a gloom over Sydney until the evening at half past six o'clock. Almost everyone was now disposed to think that the blood of an innocent man had been shed. 'The witnesses were all perjured, not excepting Mr Cox'; 'The jury were a parcel of fools'; and 'The Governor, who would not listen to the judge, a hardhearted and cruel man.' Such were the opinions that were current from one end of Sydney to the other.

But at the hour above mentioned – half past six in the evening – the public mind was disabused of its erroneous idea. At that hour it became generally known that on the previous night Mr Smith had sent for the Reverend Mr Cooper, and to that gentleman had confessed that he deserved the fate that awaited him; that for more than two years he had contemplated the murder of John Fisher, for the sake of his wealth, which was equal to twenty thousand pounds; that the man who had personated Fisher, and executed the power of attorney, had gone to England, and written thence the letter upon which he so much relied in his defence, was a convict who resembled the deceased in person, and to whom he (Smith) gave Fisher's certificate of freedom; that it was his (Smith's) intention to have left the Colony as soon as the proceeds of the sale came into his possession – partly because he longed to lead the last portion of his life in England, but chiefly because, from the day on which he committed the murder, he had been haunted by that ghost which old Weir had truly sworn he saw sitting on the rail; that the deed was done by a single blow from a tomahawk, and that the deceased never spoke after it was inflicted. He protested that the man who had personated Fisher, in respect to the execution of the power of attorney, and who had escaped from the Colony, was ignorant of his (Smith's) intention to murder Fisher; and that the letter which had been forwarded from England was only a copy of one which he (Smith) had told him to despatch a few months after he had arrived at home. He concluded by saying, that since he struck Fisher that fatal blow his life had been a burden to him, much as he had struggled to disguise his feelings, and put a bold front on the matter; and that he would much rather, since he had been convicted, suffer death than be reprieved – although he hoped that until after the breath had left his body, his confession would be kept a secret.

7 The House of Death

It is important to remember that in the majority of cases ghosts harm no one. Most hauntings are only frightening to ordinary mortals because we cannot understand what is going on. And anything we do not understand tends to frighten us. Fiction writers make a great deal of malicious ghosts, the kind that are supposed to intend evil against living people. They are scarce in real life.

Here is one, however, a strange case that combines features often found in haunted houses, and some which, thank goodness, are rare. Like the story in Chapter Five, it was first published in *The Tatler* magazine, where it was signed only with the author's initials.

SEVEN YEARS IN A HAUNTED HOUSE
by J. F. O'C.

Strange as this narrative may appear, it is an absolutely true account of a house haunted by ghosts, in which I my parents, and other members of our family lived, I am sorry to say – and I have reason for saying it – during seven years. The house in question, No. 22, was idle for some time, when my father, who was on the look-out for a residence in the City, convenient to his business, took it.

Shortly after moving in we heard strange noises, always in the evening and at night, in the basement, which consisted of two kitchens, front and back, scullery, etc. None of us seemed to pay attention to these noises at first, but one night, about nine p.m., while sitting in the study with my father and mother, the noises were, to say the least of it, disturbing. My father spoke, 'Go down,' he said to me, 'and tell the girl to stop chopping those sticks. I gave orders all firewood was to be broken at the store' (his place of business).

I obeyed. On the stairs, going down, the noise ceased. I went into the kitchen, the gas was lighted low, but there was no one there. The kitchen maid was out – her night off – the other was upstairs at the top of the house.

When I returned to the study I said nothing, and fortunately no remark was made, but about an hour after, the noise commenced again. This time my father went down, with the same result. When he came back he said nothing, but looked at me, I thought, curiously.

After a while, I prepared to retire (I was then in my teens). On the way up I tripped on the stairs. My father came out and helped me to my room. I told him I *felt* as if someone knocked me on the stairs, but that I saw no one there.

'Did you see anyone in the kitchen?' he asked.

'No,' I answered, 'there was no one there either.'

'Say nothing of this,' he said. 'Leave things to me.'

These noises, as of wood-chopping, went on at night, and strangely enough, as we noticed in time, always on the thirtieth day of the month. It was my father who noted this first, and need I say both he and I looked forward to that day with anxiety. I do not know what my mother thought; she never spoke of it to us, nor we to her.

Some time after this, my elder and only brother returned from school, and my eldest sister from a boarding school. The house was five storeys high, and my brother and I occupied a back bedroom on the third storey, a door leading from it into my father's, in the front. My sister, with her younger sister for company, slept in the back drawing-room, which was occasionally the visitors' room; this comprised the whole family at the time.

One night on my way to bed, with my candle and the gas lighted on the landing outside the drawing-room, I stopped to close the door which had been left open, as likewise my sister's, when I distinctly saw a tall woman, dressed in brown, come out of the drawing-room and enter my sister's room. I thought it strange, and I followed her. There was a candle lighted in the room, and my young sister was asleep. This woman – I cannot call it anything else – walked round the bed, looked at my sister, then at me, put up her two arms, and disappeared. I dropped my candlestick, gave a shout, and fell. When I recovered consciousness I was on the floor, with a pillow under my head; they were bathing my forehead, and my young sister was sitting up terribly frightened.

Next day I told my father privately what I saw, and then my eldest sister asked me. I tried to pass it off.

' 'Tis no use,' she said, 'this house is haunted. You must have seen the woman in brown. Frequently,' she continued, 'every stitch of the bedclothes is swept off us and thrown over into the corner near the window. I keep a candle lighted all night, but although I saw nothing, I think my young sister suspects there is something wrong.'

The next thing happened on Christmas Eve. It was the custom for all the family, maids included, to go up to my father's bedroom at six p.m., and there he lit the Christmas candle (an old Irish custom). On this occasion he was the last going up, and he told me afterwards he distinctly saw a tall woman in brown come out of the drawing-room. 'I followed her in,' he said, 'and put my foot on her train, but there was nothing to catch. She went to the corner, put up her hand, and disappeared.'

He described her. She was identical with what I and my sister had seen. My father, I may mention, was a man of iron nerve.

One night I distinctly heard someone knocking at my door; it woke me. I lit the candle (on the table between the two beds), reached out, pulled his bedclothes, and awoke my brother. I told him what I heard.

'Nonsense,' he said, 'you're dreaming!'

'I wish I was,' I answered, 'but it would be better for both of us if you were honest. I can see now you heard it too, and you were awake when I lit the candle.'

'Go to sleep,' he said, and blew out the light.

Shortly after, the knocking came again, and I heard my father's door open. I heard him go downstairs and return. The following day he asked me if I was out of my room during the night. I said 'No,' but told him what occurred.

'I heard it,' he said, 'that knocking, and I got up, lit my candle, turned the key, and when the knocking started again, opened the door, just on the knock, but there was no one there. I then went down, and someone passed me on the stairs when I was coming back. I *saw* her,' he continued, 'and put out my hand, but there was nothing. Be careful,' he went on, 'lest your mother should know anything of this – it would kill her. Leave it to me, I will get it stopped.'

Some time after this, my father went by early train one morning about twenty-five miles into the country (the next county), and returned bringing with him a very old priest, Father S. He was over eighty, on the retired list, and what is called an exorcist, one having special faculties for driving out evil spirits. To put it shortly, this old priest said Mass the following morning, and the poor old man sprinkled holy water, and recited prayers from the top of the house to the basement. Yes, I remember it well; he even went out into the coal vaults. My father accompanied him to his house again by train.

I don't know why or how, but after that we all seemed to feel more at ease. I say seemed, because, strange as it is, at times we looked at each other, yet said nothing; it seemed as if there was a kind of understanding between us, as if a look was sufficient.

The next incident that occurred baffles me. I can offer no explanation. Going up to bed one night, I was tripped on the stairs and actually thrown down. I hurt my knee. The doctor painted it with iodine, and bandaged it. I was confined to bed. Three nights afterwards, the thirtieth of the month (we made a careful note of dates, at least my father did in his diary), about nine p.m., I was in a slight sleep when I was awakened by a terrible noise on my door, something awful. A nightlight was burning in the room. I got out of bed; the hammering was terrific on the door, and my father chasing up the stairs and calling 'Stop it! Stop it!' – he actually threw off his slippers to get up quickly. 'Open the door,' he demanded. I unlocked but could not open it, and the hammering was still going on.

He came through his room into mine. I was standing in my night attire on the floor. The hammering had ceased. He went to the door. 'My good God protect us,' he said. 'Did *you* do that?'

'Father,' I said, 'I did nothing. I only got out of bed when I heard the noise and you calling.'

'Hush,' he answered, 'your mother is coming, leave all to me.'

The door was *nailed*; there were over thirty nails in it, and there was not a single nail or hammer of any description in the room!

My mother came in. 'He is not well,' said my father; 'his head is bad, get him to bed.' He then took my mother away; she was crying. He came back afterwards with a pincers, and drew all the nails. 'We never had a nail like these,' he said. 'This is terrible, it will kill your mother.'

She took to her bed next day, and the doctor said it was the heart.

A great lady friend of my mother, who frequently came to town and stayed with us, gave up staying with us. She came in as usual, but slept in the hotel at the lower end of the street. She told me that not for any money would she spend a night in the house. 'The bedclothes,' she said, 'were pulled off me and thrown in the corner of the room. When I first felt it, and felt there was someone in the room, I held them, but they were pulled – actually dragged out of my hands!'

A priest, Father A. J. S., my father's greatest friend, followed suit, he too stayed at G.'s hotel. He frequently said Mass in different rooms on different occasions, and he advised my father to leave the house at any cost.

My father then went again to the country and brought back with him old Father S. This poor and feeble old man repeated what he had previously done, even from the top to the basement. No use; things seemed, if anything, to get worse. Father A. J. S. died shortly after this, and strange to say, on the thirtieth of the month. I remember it well; I was at his funeral with my father and brother.

Shortly after his death my father told me he intended to leave the house. He went to the agent, Mr H, a cousin of my mother, and next day I noticed that he had four of his workmen ripping up the flagging in the little garden at the back. They had long poles with hooks and were dragging a big well – it was really a cesspool. They found nothing. He had two strong axle-trees put over it and a double flagging, and closed in. The agent told him privately that a murder with which a woman was connected was committed in No. 22, but he could not, or would not, give further particulars, but as far as records showed, the murder took place on the thirtieth of the month.

We left 22 and went to 25, three doors farther up on the same side. I met an old employee of my father after we moved. 'It took a great weight off my mind,' he said, 'when ye left that house, No. 22.'

'Why?' I asked, 'what do you know of it, Peter?'

'Well,' he said, 'I am an old man. I know that house for years, and never a family lived in it but the father or mother died shortly after leaving it. None of them stayed there long. And what's more,' he added, 'they all lost their money and business. God grant it doesn't happen in your father's case, for I am very fond of him.'

Well, unfortunately, I am sorry to say it did happen. Very soon after leaving, my mother died – on the thirtieth of the month (30 January). We then left 25 and returned to the first house we had, beside the business – the house I was born in. There my young sister died suddenly of heart disease, on the thirtieth of the month. Business went down, and shortly after we lost everything we had, even to the toys I played with as a child – all went under the sheriff's hammer. No use going into details, which are only too painfully true. Shortly after, my father died of a broken heart, in very reduced circumstances, and afterwards my brother, both on the thirtieth of the month; even now I dread the thirtieth of the month myself.

8 Fact or Fiction?

Up to this point all the stories, except the first, have been based on fact. Their authors claimed that the events they recounted actually happened to living people. Of course, that does not mean every detail is accurate and capable of being proved. On the contrary, the problem with ghosts is that no one has ever been able to prove they exist at all; just as no one has ever been able to prove that they do not.

Readers who want to explore the fact and fiction of ghosts and psychic phenomena might find the following books interesting and useful as well as entertaining:

Dennis BARDENS, *Ghosts and Hauntings*, The Zeus Press, 1965.

Sir Ernest BENNETT, *Apparitions and Haunted Houses*, Faber, 1939.

Aidan CHAMBERS, *Aidan Chambers' Book of Ghosts and Hauntings*, Kestrel Books, 1973.

Andrew MACKENZIE, *Apparitions and Ghosts*, Arthur Barker, 1971.

Eric RUSSELL, *Ghosts*, Batsford, 1970.

G. N. M. TYRRELL, *Apparitions*, Duckworth, revised edition 1953.

The two stories that follow are both fictional. They are the inventions of writers who, like myself, find as much to interest and entertain them in the ghosts that haunt their imaginations as they do in the spectres that walk the earth. *The Voice in the Night* is as much a horror story as it is a ghost tale; the atmosphere is gruesomely built up. *School for the Unspeakable* is one of those stories that takes ordinary ghosts and turns them into terrifying instruments of fear and evil – or was it all just a nightmare dreamed by the hero, Bart Setwick?

9 The Voice in the Night
A fiction story by W. H. Hodgson

It was a dark, starless night. We were becalmed in the Northern Pacific. Our exact position I do not know; for the sun had been hidden during the course of a weary, breathless week, by a thin haze which had seemed to float above us, about the height of our mastheads, at whiles descending and shrouding the surrounding sea.

With there being no wind, we had steadied the tiller, and I was the only man on deck. The crew, consisting of two men and a boy, were sleeping forrard in their den; while Will – my friend, and the master of our little craft – was aft in his bunk on the port side of the little cabin.

Suddenly, from out of the surrounding darkness, there came a hail:

'Schooner, ahoy!'

The cry was so unexpected that I gave no immediate answer, because of my surprise.

It came again – a voice curiously throaty and inhuman, calling from somewhere upon the dark sea away on our port broadside:

'Schooner, ahoy!'

'Hullo!' I sung out, having gathered my wits somewhat. 'What are you? What do you want?'

'You need not be afraid,' answered the queer voice, having probably noticed some trace of confusion in my tone. 'I am only an old – man.'

The pause sounded oddly; but it was only afterwards that it came back to me with any significance.

'Why don't you come alongside, then?' I queried somewhat snappishly; for I liked not his hinting at my having been a trifle shaken.

'I – I – can't. It wouldn't be safe. I—' The voice broke off, and there was silence.

'What do you mean?' I asked, growing more and more astonished. 'Why not safe? Where are you?'

I listened for a moment; but there came no answer. And then, a sudden indefinite suspicion, of I knew not what, coming to me, I stepped swiftly to the binnacle, and took out the lighted lamp. At the same time, I knocked on the deck with my heel to waken Will. Then I was back at the side, throwing the yellow funnel of light out into the silent immensity beyond our rail. As I did so, I heard a slight, muffled cry, and then the sound of a splash as though someone had dipped oars abruptly. Yet I cannot say that I saw anything with certainty; save, it seemed to me, that with the first flash of the light, there had been something upon the waters, where now there was nothing.

'Hullo, there!' I called. 'What foolery is this!'

But there came only the indistinct sounds of a boat being pulled away into the night.

Then I heard Will's voice, from the direction of the after scuttle:

'What's up, George?'

'Come here, Will!' I said.

'What is it?' he asked, coming across the deck.

I told him the queer thing which had happened. He put several questions; then, after a moment's silence, he raised his hands to his lips, and hailed:

'Boat, ahoy!'

From a long distance away there came back to us a faint reply, and my companion repeated his call. Presently, after a short period of silence, there grew on our hearing the muffled sound of oars; at which Will hailed again.

This time there was a reply:

'Put away the light.'

'I'm damned if I will,' I muttered; but Will told me to do as the voice bade, and I shoved it down under the bulwarks.

'Come nearer,' he said, and the oar strokes continued. Then, when apparently some half dozen fathoms distant, they again ceased.

'Come alongside,' exclaimed Will. 'There's nothing to be frightened of aboard here!'

'Promise that you will not show the light?'

'What's to do with you,' I burst out, 'that you're so infernally afraid of the light?'

'Because—' began the voice, and stopped short.

'Because what?' I asked quickly.

Will put his hand on my shoulder.

'Shut up a minute, old man,' he said, in a low voice. 'Let me tackle him.'

He leant more over the rail.

'See here, mister,' he said, 'this is a pretty queer business, you coming upon us like this, right out in the middle of the blessed Pacific. How are we to know what sort of a hanky-panky trick you're up to? You say there's only one of you. How are we to know, unless we get a squint at you – eh? What's your objection to the light, anyway?'

As he finished, I heard the noise of the oars again, and then the voice came; but now from a greater distance, and sounding extremely hopeless and pathetic.

'I am sorry – sorry! I would not have troubled you, only I am hungry, and – so is she.'

The voice died away, and the sound of the oars, dipping irregularly, was borne to us.

'Stop!' sung out Will. 'I don't want to drive you

away. Come back! We'll keep the light hidden, if you don't like it.'

He turned to me:

'It's a damned queer rig, this; but I think there's nothing to be afraid of?'

There was a question in his tone, and I replied:

'No, I think the poor devil's been wrecked around here, and gone crazy.'

The sound of the oars drew nearer.

'Shove that lamp back in the binnacle,' said Will; then he leaned over the rail and listened. I replaced the lamp, and came back to his side. The dipping of the oars ceased some dozen yards distant.

'Won't you come alongside now?' asked Will in an even voice. 'I have had the lamp put back in the binnacle.'

'I – I cannot,' replied the voice. 'I dare not come nearer. I dare not even pay you for the – provisions.'

'That's all right,' said Will, and hesitated. 'You're welcome to as much grub as you can take—' Again he hesitated.

'You are very good,' exclaimed the voice. 'May God, Who understands everything, reward you—' It broke off huskily.

'The – the lady?' said Will abruptly. 'Is she—'

'I have left her behind upon the island,' came the voice.

'What island?' I cut in.

'I know not its name,' returned the voice. 'I would to God—!' it began, and checked itself as suddenly.

'Could we not send a boat for her?' asked Will at this point.

'No!' said the voice, with extraordinary emphasis. 'My God! No!' There was a moment's pause; then it added, in a tone which seemed a merited reproach:

'It was because of our want I ventured — because her agony tortured me.'

'I am a forgetful brute,' exclaimed Will. 'Just wait a minute, whoever you are, and I will bring you up something at once.'

In a couple of minutes he was back again, and his arms were full of various edibles. He paused at the rail.

'Can't you come alongside for them?' he asked.

'No — I *dare not*,' replied the voice, and it seemed to me that in its tones I detected a note of stifled craving — as though the owner hushed a mortal desire. It came to me then in a flash, that the poor old creature out there in the darkness was *suffering* for actual need of that which Will held in his arms; and yet, because of some unintelligible dread, refraining from dashing to the side of our little schooner and receiving it. And with the lightning-like conviction, there came the knowledge that the Invisible was not mad; but sanely facing some intolerable horror.

'Damn it, Will!' I said, full of many feelings, over which predominated a vast sympathy. 'Get a box. We must float off the stuff to him in it.'

This we did — propelling it away from the vessel, out into the darkness, by means of a boathook. In a minute, a slight cry from the Invisible came to us, and we knew that he had secured the box.

A little later, he called out a farewell to us, and so heartful a blessing that I am sure we were the better for it. Then, without more ado, we heard the ply of oars across the darkness.

'Pretty soon off,' remarked Will, with perhaps just a little sense of injury.

'Wait,' I replied. 'I think somehow he'll come back. He must have been badly needing that food.'

'And the lady,' said Will. For a moment he was silent; then he continued:

'It's the queerest thing ever I've tumbled across, since I've been fishing.'

'Yes,' I said, and fell to pondering.

And so the time slipped away – an hour, another, and still Will stayed with me; for the queer adventure had knocked all desire for sleep out of him.

The third hour was three parts through, when we heard again the sound of oars across the silent ocean.

'Listen!' said Will, a low note of excitement in his voice.

'He's coming, just as I thought,' I muttered.

The dipping of the oars grew nearer, and I noted that the strokes were firmer and longer. The food had been needed.

They came to a stop a little distance off the broadside, and the queer voice came again to us through the darkness:

'Schooner, ahoy!'

'That you?' asked Will.

'Yes,' replied the voice. 'I left you suddenly; but – but there was great need.'

'The lady?' questioned Will.

'The – lady is grateful now on earth. She will be more grateful soon in – in heaven.'

Will began to make some reply, in a puzzled voice; but became confused, and broke off short. I said nothing. I was wondering at the curious pauses, and, apart from my wonder, I was full of a great sympathy.

The voice continued:

'We – she and I, have talked, as we shared the result of God's tenderness and yours—'

Will interposed; but without coherence.

'I beg of you not to – to belittle your deed of Christian charity this night,' said the voice. 'Be sure that it has not escaped His notice.'

It stopped, and there was a full minute's silence. Then it came again:

'We have spoken together upon that which – which has befallen us. We had thought to go out, without telling any, of the terror which has come into our – lives. She is with me in believing that tonight's happenings are under a special ruling, and that it is God's wish that we should tell to you all that we have suffered since – since—'

'Yes?' said Will softly.

'Since the sinking of the *Albatross*.'

'Ah!' I exclaimed involuntarily. 'She left Newcastle for 'Frisco some six months ago, and hasn't been heard of since.'

'Yes,' answered the voice. 'But some few degrees to the north of the line she was caught in a terrible storm, and dismasted. When the day came, it was found that she was leaking badly, and, presently, it falling to a calm, the sailors took to the boats, leaving – leaving a young lady – my fiancée – and myself upon the wreck.

'We were below, gathering together a few of our belongings, when they left. They were entirely callous, through fear, and when we came up upon the decks, we saw them only as small shapes afar off upon the horizon. Yet we did not despair, but set to work and constructed a small raft. Upon this we put such few matters as it would hold, including a quantity of water and some ship's biscuit. Then, the vessel being very deep in the water, we got ourselves on to the raft, and pushed off.

'It was later, when I observed that we seemed to be in the way of some tide or current, which bore us from the ship at an angle; so that in the course of three hours, by my watch, her hull became invisible to our sight, her broken masts remaining in view for a somewhat longer period. Then, toward evening, it grew misty, and so through the night. The next day we were still encompassed by the mist, the weather remaining quiet.

'For four days we drifted through this strange haze, until, on the evening of the fourth day, there grew upon our ears the murmur of breakers at a distance. Gradually it became plainer, and, somewhat after midnight, it appeared to sound upon either hand at no very great space. The raft was raised upon a swell several times, and then we were in smooth water, and the noise of the breakers was behind.

'When the morning came, we found that we were in a sort of great lagoon; but of this we noticed little at the time; for close before us, through the enshrouding mist, loomed the hull of a large sailing-vessel. With one accord, we fell upon our knees and thanked God; for we thought that here was an end to our perils. We had much to learn.

'The raft drew near to the ship, and we shouted on them to take us aboard; but none answered. Presently the raft touched against the side of the vessel, and, seeing a rope hanging downwards, I seized it and began to climb. Yet I had much ado to make my way up, because of a kind of grey, lichenous fungus which had seized upon the rope, and which blotched the side of the ship lividly.

'I reached the rail and clambered over it, on to the

deck. Here I saw that the decks were covered, in great patches, with the grey masses, some of them rising into nodules several feet in height; but at the time I thought less of this matter than of the possibility of here being people aboard the ship. I shouted; but none answered. Then I went to the door below the poop deck. I opened it, and peered in. There was a great smell of staleness, so that I knew in a moment that nothing living was within, and with the knowledge, I shut the door quickly; for I felt suddenly lonely.

'I went back to the side where I had scrambled up. My – my sweetheart was still sitting quietly upon the raft. Seeing me look down she called up to know whether there were any aboard of the ship. I replied that the vessel had the appearance of having been long deserted; but that if she would wait a little I would see whether there was anything in the shape of a ladder by which she could ascend to the deck. Then we would make a search through the vessel together. A little later, on the opposite side of the decks, I found a rope side-ladder. This I carried across, and a minute afterwards she was beside me.

'Together we explored the cabins and apartments in the after part of the ship; but nowhere was there any sign of life. Here and there, within the cabins themselves, we came across odd patches of that queer fungus; but this, as my sweetheart said, could be cleaned away.

'In the end, having assured ourselves that the after portion of the vessel was empty, we picked our ways to the bows, between the ugly grey nodules of that strange growth; and here we made a further search, which told us that there was indeed none aboard but ourselves.

'This being now beyond any doubt, we returned to

the stern of the ship and proceeded to make ourselves as comfortable as possible. Together we cleared out and cleaned two of the cabins; and after that I made examination whether there was anything eatable in the ship. This I soon found was so, and thanked God in my heart for His goodness. In addition to this I discovered the whereabouts of the freshwater pump, and having fixed it I found the water drinkable, though somewhat unpleasant to the taste.

'For several days we stayed aboard the ship, without attempting to get to the shore. We were busily engaged in making the place habitable. Yet even thus early we became aware that our lot was even less to be desired than might have been imagined; for though, as a first I saw the thing upon her pillow I shuddered, and then studded the floors and walls of the cabins and saloon, yet they returned almost to their original size within the space of twenty-four hours, which not only discouraged us, but gave us a feeling of vague unease.

'Still we would not admit ourselves beaten, so set to work afresh, and not only scraped away the fungus, but soaked the places where it had been, with carbolic, a canful of which I had found in the pantry. Yet, by the end of the week the growth had returned in full strength, and, in addition, it had spread to other places, as though our touching it had allowed germs from it to travel elsewhere.

'On the seventh morning, my sweetheart woke to find a small patch of it growing on her pillow, close to her face. At that, she came to me, so soon as she could get her garments upon her. I was in the galley at the time lighting the fire for breakfast.

' "Come here, John," she said, and led me aft. When I saw the thing up her pillow I shuddered, and then and there we agreed to go right out of the ship and see whether we could not fare to make ourselves more comfortable ashore.

'Hurriedly we gathered together our few belongings, and even among these I found that the fungus had been at work; for one of her shawls had a little lump of it growing near one edge. I threw the whole thing over the side, without saying anything to her.

'The raft was still alongside, but it was too clumsy to guide, and I lowered down a small boat that hung across the stern, and in this we made our way to the shore. Yet, as we drew near to it, I became gradually aware that here the vile fungus, which had driven us from the ship, was growing riot. In places it rose into horrible, fantastic mounds, which seemed almost to quiver, as with a quiet life, when the wind blew across them. Here and there it took on the forms of vast fingers, and in others it just spread out flat and smooth and treacherous. Odd places, it appeared as grotesque stunted trees, seeming extraordinarily kinked and gnarled – the whole quaking vilely at times.

'At first, it seemed to us that there was no single portion of the surrounding shore which was not hidden beneath the masses of the hideous lichen; yet, in this, I found we were mistaken; for somewhat later, coasting along the shore at a little distance, we descried a smooth white patch of what appeared to be fine sand, and there we landed. It was not sand. What it was I do not know. All that I have observed is that upon it the fungus will not grow; while everywhere else, save where the sand-like earth wanders oddly, pathwise, amid the grey desolation of the lichen, there is nothing but that loathsome greyness.

'It is difficult to make you understand how cheered

we were to find one place that was absolutely free from the growth, and here we deposited our belongings. Then we went back to the ship for such things as it seemed to us we should need. Among other matters, I managed to bring ashore with me one of the ship's sails, with which I constructed two small tents, which, though exceedingly rough-shaped, served the purposes for which they were intended. In these we lived and stored our various necessities, and thus for a matter of some four weeks all went smoothly and without partcular unhappiness. Indeed, I may say with much of happiness – for – for we were together.

'It was on the thumb of her right hand that the growth first showed. It was only a small circular spot, much like a little grey mole. My God! how the fear leapt to my heart when she showed me the place. We cleansed it, between us, washing it with carbolic and water. In the morning of the following day she showed her hand to me again. The grey warty thing had returned. For a little while, we looked at one another in silence. Then, still wordless, we started again to remove it. In the midst of the operation she spoke suddenly.

' "What's that on the side of your face, dear?" Her voice was sharp with anxiety. I put my hand up to feel.

' "There! Under the hair by your ear. A little to the front a bit." My finger rested upon the place, and then I knew.

' "Let us get your thumb done first," I said. And she submitted, only because she was afraid to touch me until it was cleansed. I finished washing and disinfecting her thumb, and then she turned to my face. After it was finished we sat together and talked awhile of many things; for there had come into our lives sudden, very terrible thoughts. We were, all at once, afraid of something worse than death. We spoke of loading the boat with provisions and water and making our way out on to the sea; yet we were helpless, for many causes, and – and the growth had attacked us already. We decided to stay. God would do with us what was His will. We would wait.

'A month, two months, three months passed and the places grew somewhat, and there had come others. Yet we fought so strenuously with the fear that its headway was but slow, comparatively speaking.

'Occasionally we ventured off to the ship for such stores as we needed. There we found that the fungus grew persistently. One of the nodules on the maindeck became soon as high as my head.

'We had now given up all thought or hope of leaving the island. We had realised that it would be unallowable to go among healthy humans, with the things from which we were suffering.

'With this determination and knowledge in our minds we knew that we should have to husband our food and water; for we did not know, at that time, but that we should possibly live for many years.

'This reminds me that I have told you that I am an old man. Judged by years this is not so. But – but—'

He broke off; then continued somewhat abruptly:

'As I was saying, we knew that we should have to use care in the matter of food. But we had no idea then how little food there was left, of which to take care. It was a week later that I made the discovery that all the other bread tanks – which I had supposed full – were empty, and that (beyond odd tins of vegetables and meat, and some other matters) we had nothing on which to depend, but the bread in the tank which I had already opened.

'After learning this I bestirred myself to do what I could, and set to work at fishing in the lagoon; but with no success. At this I was somewhat inclined to feel desperate until the thought came to me to try outside the lagoon, in the open sea.

'Here, at times, I caught odd fish; but so infrequently that they proved of but little help in keeping us from the hunger which threatened. It seemed to me that our deaths were likely to come by hunger, and not by the growth of the thing which had seized upon our bodies.

'We were in this state of mind when the fourth month wore out. Then I made a very horrible discovery. One morning, a little before midday, I came off from the ship with a portion of the biscuits which were left. In the mouth of her tent I saw my sweetheart sitting, eating something.

' "What is it, my dear?" I called out as I leapt ashore. Yet, on hearing my voice, she seemed confused, and, turning, slyly threw something towards the edge of the little clearing. It fell short, and a vague suspicion having arisen within me, I walked across and picked it up. It was a piece of the grey fungus.

'As I went to her with it in my hand, she turned deadly pale; then a rose red.

'I felt strangely dazed and frightened.

' "My dear! My dear!" I said, and could say no more. Yet at my words she broke down and cried bitterly. Gradually, as she calmed, I got from her the news that she had tried it the preceding day, and – and liked it. I got her to promise on her knees not to touch it again, however great our hunger. After she had promised she told me that the desire for it had come suddenly, and that, until the moment of desire, she had experienced nothing towards it but the most extreme repulsion.

'Later in the day, feeling strangely restless, and much shaken with the thing which I had discovered, I made my way along one of the twisted paths – formed by the white, sand-like substance – which led among the fungoid growth. I had, once before, ventured along there; but not to any great distance. This time, being involved in perplexing thought, I went much farther than hitherto.

'Suddenly I was called to myself by a queer hoarse sound on my left. Turning quickly I saw that there was movement among an extraordinarily shaped mass of fungus, close to my elbow. It was swaying uneasily, as though it possessed life of its own. Abruptly, as I stared, the thought came to me that the thing had a grotesque resemblance to the figure of a distorted human creature. Even as the fancy flashed into my brain, there was a slight, sickening noise of tearing, and I saw that one of the branch-like arms was detaching itself from the surrounding grey masses, and coming towards me. The head of the thing – a shapeless grey ball, inclined in my direction. I stood stupidly, and the vile arm brushed across my face. I gave out a frightened cry, and ran back a few paces. There was a sweetish taste upon my lips where the thing had touched me. I licked them, and was immediately filled with an inhuman desire. I turned and seized a mass of the fungus. Then more, and – more. I was insatiable. In the midst of devouring, the remembrance of the morning's discovery swept into my mazed brain. It was sent by God. I dashed the fragment I held to the ground. Then, utterly wretched and feeling a dreadful guiltiness, I made my way back to the little encampment.

'I think she knew, by some marvellous intuition which love must have given, so soon as she set eyes on me. Her quiet sympathy made it easier for me, and I told her of my sudden weakness; yet omitted to mention the extraordinary thing which had gone before. I desired to spare her all unnecessary terror.

'But, for myself, I had added an intolerable knowledge, to breed an incessant terror in my brain; for I doubted not but that I had seen the end of one of those men who had come to the island in the ship in the lagoon; and in that monstrous ending I had seen our own.

'Thereafter we kept from the abominable food, though the desire for it had entered into our blood. Yet our drear punishment was upon us; for, day by day, with monstrous rapidity, the fungoid growth took hold of our poor bodies. Nothing we could do would check it materially, and so – and so – we who had been human, became—. Well, it matters less each day. Only – only we had been man and maid!

'And day by day, the fight is more dreadful, to withstand the hunger-lust for the terrible lichen.

'A week ago we ate the last of the biscuit, and since that time I have caught three fish. I was out here fishing tonight, when your schooner drifted upon me out of the mist. I hailed you. You know the rest, and may God, out of His great heart, bless you for your goodness to a – a couple of poor outcast souls.'

There was the dip of an oar – another. Then the voice came again, and for the last time, sounding through the slight surrounding mist, ghostly and mournful.

'God bless you! Goodbye.'

'Goodbye,' we shouted together, hoarsely, our hearts full of many emotions.

I glanced about me. I became aware that the dawn was upon us.

The sun flung a stray beam across the hidden sea; pierced the mist dully, and lit up the receding boat with a gloomy fire. Indistinctly, I saw something nodding between the oars. I thought of a sponge – a great, grey nodding sponge. The oars continued to ply. They were grey – as was the boat – and my eyes searched a moment vainly for the conjunction of hand and oar. My gaze flashed back to the – head. It nodded forward as the oars dipped, the boat shot out of the patch of light, and then – the thing went nodding into the mist.

10 School for the Unspeakable
A fiction story by Manley Wade Wellman

Bart Setwick dropped off the train at Carrington and stood for a moment on the station platform, an honest-faced, well-knit lad in tweeds. This little town and its famous school would be his home for the next eight months; but which way to the school? The sun had set, and he could barely see the shop signs across Carrington's modest main street. He hesitated, and a soft voice spoke at his very elbow.

'Are you for the school?'

Startled, Bart Setwick wheeled. In the grey twilight stood another youth, smiling thinly and waiting as if for an answer. The stranger was all of nineteen years old – that meant maturity to young Setwick, who was fifteen – and his pale face had shrewd lines to it. His tall, shambling body was clad in high-necked jersey and unfashionably tight trousers. Bart Setwick skimmed him with the quick, appraising eye of young America.

'I just got here,' he replied. 'My name's Setwick.'

'Mine's Hoag.' Out came a slender hand. Setwick took it and found it froggy-cold, with a suggestion of steel-wire muscles. 'Glad to meet you. I came down on the chance someone would drop off the train. Let me give you a lift to the school.'

Hoag turned away, felinely light for all his ungainliness, and led his new acquaintance around the corner of the little wooden railway station. Behind the structure, half hidden in its shadow, stood a shabby buggy with a lean bay horse in the shafts.

'Get in,' invited Hoag, but Bart Setwick paused for a moment. His generation was not used to such vehicles.

Hoag chuckled and said, 'Oh, this is only a school wrinkle. We run to funny customs. Get in.'

Setwick obeyed. 'How about my trunk?'

'Leave it.' The taller youth swung himself in beside Setwick and took the reins. 'You'll not need it tonight.'

He snapped his tongue and the bay horse stirred, drew them around and off down a bush-lined road. Its hoofbeats were oddly muffled.

They turned a corner, another, and came into open country. The lights of Carrington, newly kindled against the night, hung behind like a constellation settled down to Earth. Setwick felt a hint of chill that did not seem to fit the September evening.

'How far is the school from town?' he asked.

'Four or five miles,' Hoag replied in his hushed voice. 'That was deliberate on the part of the founders – they wanted to make it hard for the students to get to town for larks. It forced us to dig up our own amusements.' The pale face creased in a faint smile, as if this were a pleasantry. 'There's just a few of the right sort on hand tonight. By the way, what did you get sent out for?'

Setwick frowned his mystification. 'Why, to go to school. Dad sent me.'

'But what for? Don't you know that this is a high-class prison prep? Half of us are lunkheads that need poking along, the other half are fellows who got in scandals somewhere else. Like me.' Again Hoag smiled.

Setwick began to dislike his companion. They rolled a mile or so in silence before Hoag again asked a question:

'Do you go to church, Setwick?'

The new boy was afraid to appear priggish, and made a careless show with, 'Not very often.'

'Can you recite anything from the Bible?' Hoag's soft voice took on an anxious tinge.

'Not that I know of.'

'Good,' was the almost hearty response. 'As I was saying, there's only a few of us at the school tonight – only three, to be exact. And we don't like Bible-quoters.'

Setwick laughed, trying to appear sage and cynical. 'Isn't Satan reputed to quote the Bible to his own. . . .'

'What do you know about Satan?' interrupted Hoag. He turned full on Setwick, studying him with intent, dark eyes. Then, as if answering his own question: 'Little enough, I'll bet. Would you like to know about him?'

'Sure I would,' replied Setwick, wondering what the joke would be.

'I'll teach you after a while,' Hoag promised cryptically, and silence fell again.

Half a moon was well up as they came in sight of a dark jumble of buildings.

'Here we are,' announced Hoag, and then, throwing back his head, he emitted a wild, wordless howl that made Setwick almost jump out of the buggy. 'That's to let the others know we're coming,' he exclaimed. 'Listen!'

Back came a seeming echo of the howl, shrill, faint and eerie. The horse wavered in its muffled trot, and Hoag clucked it back into step. They turned in at a driveway well grown up in weeds, and two minutes more brought them up to the rear of the closest building. It was dim grey in the wash of moonbeams, with blank inky rectangles for windows. Nowhere was there a light, but as the buggy came to a halt Setwick saw a young head pop out of a window on the lower floor.

'Here already, Hoag?' came a high, reedy voice.

'Yes,' answered the youth at the reins, 'and I've brought a new man with me.'

Thrilling a bit to hear himself called a man, Setwick alighted.

'His name's Setwick,' went on Hoag. 'Meet Andoff, Setwick. A great friend of mine.'

Andoff flourished a hand in greeting and scrambled out over the window-sill. He was chubby and squat and even paler than Hoag, with a low forehead beneath lank, wet-looking hair, and black eyes set wide apart in a fat, stupid-looking face. His shabby jacket was too tight for him, and beneath worn trousers his legs and feet were bare. He might have been an overgrown thirteen or an underdeveloped eighteen.

'Felcher ought to be along in half a second,' he volunteered.

'Entertain Setwick while I put up the buggy,' Hoag directed him.

Andoff nodded, and Hoag gathered the lines in his hands, but paused for a final word.

'No funny business yet, Andoff,' he cautioned seriously. 'Setwick, don't let this lard-bladder rag you or tell you wild stories until I come back.'

Andoff laughed shrilly. 'No, no wild stories,' he promised. 'You'll do the talking, Hoag.'

The buggy trundled away, and Andoff swung his fat, grinning face to the new arrival.

'Here comes Felcher,' he announced. 'Felcher, meet Setwick.'

Another boy had bobbed up, it seemed, from nowhere. Setwick had not seen him come around the corner of the building, or slip out of a door or window. He was probably as old as Hoag, or older, but so small as to be almost a dwarf, and frail to boot. His most notable characteristic was his hairiness. A great mop covered his head, brushed over his neck and ears, and hung unkemptly to his bright, deep-set eyes. His lips and cheeks were spread with a rank down, and a curly thatch peeped through the unbuttoned collar of his soiled white shirt. The hand he offered Setwick was almost simian in its shagginess and in the hardness of its palm. Too, it was cold and damp. Setwick remembered the same thing of Hoag's handclasp.

'We're the only ones here so far,' Felcher remarked. His voice, surprisingly deep and strong for so small a creature, rang like a great bell.

'Isn't even the headmaster here?' inquired Setwick, and at that the other two began to laugh uproariously, Andoff's fife-squeal rendering an obbligato to Felcher's bell-boom. Hoag, returning, asked what the fun was.

'Setwick asks,' groaned Felcher, 'why the headmaster isn't here to welcome him.'

More fife-laughter and bell-laughter.

'I doubt if Setwick would think the answer was funny,' Hoag commented, and then chuckled softly himself.

Setwick, who had been well brought up, began to grow nettled.

'Tell me about it,' he urged, in what he hoped was a bleak tone, 'and I'll join your chorus of mirth.'

Felcher and Andoff gazed at him with eyes strangely eager and yearning. Then they faced Hoag.

'Let's tell him,' they both said at once, but Hoag shook his head.

'Not yet. One thing at a time. Let's have the song first.'

They began to sing. The first verse of their offering

was obscene, with no pretence of humour to redeem it. Setwick had never been squeamish, but he found himself definitely repelled. The second verse seemed less objectionable, but it hardly made sense:

> All they tried to teach here
> Now goes untaught.
> Ready, steady, each here,
> Knowledge we sought.
> What they called disaster
> Killed us not, O master!
> Rule us, we beseech here,
> Eye, hand and thought.

It was something like a hymn, Setwick decided, but before what altar would such hymns be sung? Hoag must have read that question in his mind.

'You mentioned Satan in the buggy on the way out,' he recalled, his knowing face hanging like a mask in the half dimness close to Setwick. 'Well, that was a Satanist song.'

'It was? Who made it?'

'I did,' Hoag informed him. 'How do you like it?'

Setwick made no answer. He tried to sense mockery in Hoag's voice, but could not find it. 'What,' he asked finally, 'does all this Satanist singing have to do with the headmaster?'

'A lot,' came back Felcher deeply, and 'a lot,' squealed Andoff.

Hoag gazed from one of his friends to the others, and for the first time he smiled broadly. It gave him a toothy look.

'I believe,' he ventured quietly, but weightily, 'that we might as well let Setwick in on the secret of our little circle.'

Here it would begin, the new boy decided – the school hazing of which he had heard and read so much. He had anticipated such things with something of excitement, even eagerness, but now he wanted none of them. He did not like his three companions, and he did not like the way they approached whatever it was they intended to do. He moved backward a pace or two, as if to retreat.

Swift as darting birds, Hoag and Andoff closed in at either elbow. Their chill hands clutched him and suddenly he felt light-headed and sick. Things that had been clear in the moonlight went hazy and distorted.

'Come on and sit down, Setwick,' invited Hoag, as though from a great distance. His voice did not grow loud or harsh, but it embodied real menace. 'Sit on that window-sill. Or would you like us to carry you?'

At the moment Setwick wanted only to be free of their touch, and so he walked unresistingly to the sill and scrambed up on it. Behind him was the blackness of an unknown chamber, and at his knees gathered the three who seemed so eager to tell him their private joke.

'The headmaster was a proper churchgoer,' began Hoag, as though he were the spokesman for the group. 'He didn't have any use for devils or devil-worship. Went on record against them when he addressed us in chapel. That was what started us.'

'Right,' nodded Andoff, turning up his fat, larval face. 'Anything he outlawed, we wanted to do. Isn't that logic?'

'Logic and reason,' wound up Felcher. His hairy right hand twiddled on the sill near Setwick's thigh. In the moonlight it looked like a big, nervous spider.

Hoag resumed, 'I don't know of any prohibition of his it was easier or more fun to break.'

Setwick found that his mouth had gone dry. His tongue could barely moisten his lips. 'You mean,' he said, 'that you began to worship devils?'

Hoag nodded happily, like a teacher at an apt pupil. 'One vacation I got a book on the cult. The three of us studied it, then began ceremonies. We learned the charms and spells, forward and backward. . . .'

'They're twice as good backward,' put in Felcher, and Andoff giggled.

'Have you any idea, Setwick,' Hoag almost cooed, 'what it was that appeared in our study the first time we burned wine and sulphur, with the proper words spoken over them?'

Setwick did not want to know. He clenched his teeth. 'If you're trying to scare me,' he managed to growl out, 'it certainly isn't going to work.'

All three laughed once more, and began to chatter out their protestations of good faith.

'I swear that we're telling the truth, Setwick,' Hoag assured him. 'Do you want to hear it, or don't you?'

Setwick had very little choice in the matter, and he realised it. 'Oh, go ahead,' he capitulated, wondering how it would do to crawl backward from the sill into the darkness of the room.

Hoag leaned toward him, with the air as of one confiding. 'The headmaster caught us. Caught us red-handed.'

'Book open, fire burning,' chanted Felcher.

'He had something very fine to say about the vengeance of heaven,' Hoag went on. 'We got to laughing at him. He worked up a frenzy. Finally he tried to take heaven's vengeance into his own hands – tried to visit it on us, in a very primitive way. But it didn't work.'

Andoff was laughing immoderately, his fat arms across his bent belly.

'He thought it worked,' he supplemented between high gurgles, 'but it didn't.'

'Nobody could kill us,' Felcher added. 'Not after the oaths we'd taken, and the promises that had been made us.'

'What promises?' demanded Setwick, who was struggling hard not to believe. 'Who made you any promises?'

'Those we worshipped,' Felcher told him. If he was simulating earnestness, it was a supreme bit of acting. Setwick, realising this, was more daunted than he cared to show.

'When did all these things happen?' was his next question.

'When?' echoed Hoag. 'Oh, years and years ago.'

'Years and years ago,' repeated Andoff.

'Long before you were born,' Felcher assured him.

They were standing close together, their backs to the moon that shone in Setwick's face. He could not see their expressions clearly. But their three voices – Hoag's soft, Felcher's deep and vibrant, Andoff's high and squeaky – were absolutely serious.

'I know what you're arguing within yourself,' Hoag announced somewhat smugly. 'How can we, who talk about those many past years, seem so young? That calls for an explanation, I'll admit.' He paused, as if choosing words. 'Time – for us – stands still. It came to a halt on that very night, Setwick; the night our headmaster tried to put an end to our worship.'

'And to us,' smirked the gross-bodied Andoff, with his usual air of self-congratulation at capping one of Hoag's statements.

'The worship goes on,' pronounced Felcher, in the same chanting manner that he had affected once before. 'The worship goes on, and we go on, too.'

'Which brings us to the point,' Hoag came in briskly. 'Do you want to throw in with us, Setwick? – make the fourth of this lively little party?'

'No, I don't,' snapped Setwick vehemently.

They fell silent, and gave back a little – a trio of bizarre silhouettes against the pale moonglow. Setwick could see the flash of their staring eyes among the shadows of their faces. He knew that he was afraid, but hid his fear. Pluckily he dropped from the sill to the ground. Dew from the grass spattered his sock-clad ankles between oxfords and trouser cuffs.

'I guess it's my turn to talk,' he told them levelly. 'I'll make it short. I don't like you, nor anything you've said. And I'm getting out of here.'

'We won't let you,' said Hoag, hushed but emphatic.

'We won't let you,' murmured Andoff and Felcher together, as though they had rehearsed it a thousand times.

Setwick clenched his fists. His father had taught him to box. He took a quick, smooth stride toward Hoag and hit him hard in the face. Next moment all three had flung themselves upon him. They did not seem to strike or grapple or tug, but he went down under their assault. The shoulders of his tweed coat wallowed in sand, and he smelled crushed weeds. Hoag, on top of him, pinioned his arms with a knee on each bicep. Felcher and Andoff were stooping close.

Glaring up in helpless rage, Setwick knew once and for all that this was no schoolboy prank. Never did practical jokers gather around their victim with such staring, green-gleaming eyes, such drawn jowls, such quivering lips.

Hoag bared white fangs. His pointed tongue quested once over them.

'Knife!' he muttered, and Felcher fumbled in a pocket, then passed him something that sparkled in the moonlight.

Hoag's lean hand reached for it, then whipped back. Hoag had lifted his eyes to something beyond the huddle. He choked and whimpered inarticulately, sprang up from Setwick's labouring chest, and fell back in awkward haste. The others followed his shocked stare, then as suddenly cowered and retreated in turn.

'It's the master!' wailed Andoff.

'Yes,' roared a gruff new voice. 'Your old headmaster – and I've come back to master you!'

Rising upon one elbow, the prostrate Setwick saw what they had seen – a tall, thick-bodied figure in a long dark coat, topped with a square, distorted face and a tousle of white locks. Its eyes glittered with their own pale, hard light. As it advanced slowly and heavily it emitted a snigger of murderous joy. Even at first glance Setwick was aware that it cast no shadow.

'I am in time,' mouthed the newcomer. 'You were going to kill this poor boy.'

Hoag had recovered and made a stand. 'Kill him?' he quavered, seeming to fawn before the threatening presence. 'No. We'd have given him life—'

'You call it life!' trumpeted the long-coated one. 'You'd have sucked out his blood to teem your own dead veins, damned him to your filthy condition. But I'm here to prevent you!'

A finger pointed, huge and knuckly, and then came a

torrent of language. To the nerve-stunned Setwick it sounded like a bit from the New Testament, or perhaps from the Book of Common Prayer. All at once he remembered Hoag's avowed dislike for such quotations.

His three erstwhile assailants reeled as if before a high wind that chilled or scorched. 'No, no! Don't!' they begged wretchedly.

The square old face gaped open and spewed merciless laughter. The knuckly finger traced a cross in the air, and the trio wailed in chorus as though the sign had been drawn upon their flesh with a tongue of flame.

Hoag dropped to his knees. 'Don't!' he sobbed.

'I have power,' mocked their tormentor. 'During years shut up I won it, and now I'll use it.' Again a triumphant burst of mirth. 'I know you're damned and can't be killed, but you can be tortured! I'll make you crawl like worms before I'm done with you!'

Setwick gained his shaky feet. The long coat and the blocky head leaned toward him.

'Run, you!' dinned a rough roar in his ears. 'Get out of here – and thank God for the chance!'

Setwick ran, staggering. He blundered through the weeds of the driveway, gained the road beyond. In the distance gleamed the lights of Carrington. As he turned his face toward them and quickened his pace he began to weep, chokingly, hysterically, exhaustingly.

He did not stop running until he reached the platform in front of the station. A clock across the street struck ten, in a deep voice not unlike Felcher's. Setwick breathed deeply, fished out his handkerchief and mopped his face. His hand was quivering like a grass stalk in a breeze.

'Beg pardon!' came a cheery hail. 'You must be Setwick.'

As once before on this same platform, he whirled around with startled speed. Within touch of him stood a broad-shouldered man of thirty or so, with horn-rimmed spectacles. He wore a neat Norfolk jacket and flannels. A short briar pipe was clamped in a good-humoured mouth.

'I'm Collins, one of the masters at the school,' he introduced himself. 'If you're Setwick, you've had us worried. We expected you on that seven o'clock train, you know. I dropped down to see if I couldn't trace you.'

Setwick found a little of his lost wind. 'But I've – been to the school,' he mumbled protestingly. His hand, still trembling, gestured vaguely along the way he had come.

Collins threw back his head and laughed, then apologised.

'Sorry,' he said. 'It's no joke if you really had all that walk for nothing. Why, that old place is deserted – used to be a catch-all for incorrigible rich boys. They closed it about fifty years ago, when the headmaster went mad and killed three of his pupils. As a matter of coincidence, the master himself died just this afternoon, in the state hospital for the insane.'

More TOPLINERS for your enjoyment

Escapers
Compiled by Aidan Chambers
True accounts of men who attempted to escape from captivity during the Second World War. Stories of men digging tunnels, hijacking an aeroplane, disguising themselves, joining resistance fighters: using every ounce of their ingenuity, determination and courage.

I Want to Stay Here!
Christine Dickenson
When Sue's family decide to emigrate, she refuses to leave home. She wants to be a vet and has a job she likes in the local animal surgery. This is the story of how she gets her way and begins life alone for the first time at 17.

Vicky Takes a Chance
Jenny Hewitt
Fifteen-year-old Vicky starts shoplifting apparently for fun. But of course she gets caught. Her family and boyfriend are upset and she takes the chance that comes her way in approved school.

The editor of Topliners is always pleased to hear what readers think of the books and to receive ideas for new titles. If you want to write to him, please address your letter to: The Editor, Topliners, Macmillan, Houndmills, Basingstoke, Hampshire RG21 2XS. All letters received will be answered.

TOPLINERS published by Macmillan